THE GUARDIANS *of* GA'HOOLE

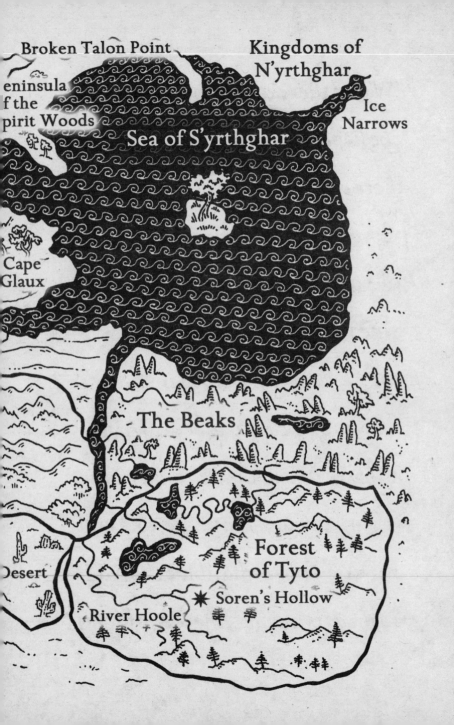

Broken Talon Point

Kingdoms of
N'yrthghar

Peninsula
of the
Spirit Woods

Ice
Narrows

Sea of S'yrthghar

Cape
Glaux

The Beaks

Desert

Forest
of Tyto

Soren's Hollow

River Hoole

"Where there are legends, there can be hope. Where there are legends, there can be dreams of knightly owls, from a kingdom called Ga'Hoole, who will rise each night into the blackness and perform noble deeds. Owls who speak no words but true ones. Owls whose only purpose is to right all wrongs, to make strong the weak, mend the broken, vanquish the proud, and make powerless those who abuse the frail. With hearts sublime, they take flight...."

GUARDIANS
of GA'HOOLE
THE LEGENDS

BOOK ELEVEN

To Be a King

BY KATHRYN LASKY

SCHOLASTIC INC.

New York Toronto London Auckland
Sydney Mexico City New Delhi Hong Kong

The author wishes to acknowledge her great debt to William Shakespeare. In Chapter 26, Hoole's address to his troops was based upon King Henry's rousing speech to his soldiers before battle in the play Henry V, *acts 3 and 4, scenes 1 and 3 respectively.*

No part of this publication may be reproduced, or stored in a retrieval system, or transmitted in any form or by any means, electronic, mechanical, photocopying, recording, or otherwise, without written permission of the publisher. For information regarding permission, write to Scholastic Inc., Attention: Permissions Department, 557 Broadway, New York, NY 10012.

ISBN 978-0-439-79570-8

Text copyright © 2006 by Kathryn Lasky.

Illustrations copyright © 2006 by Scholastic Inc. All rights reserved. Published by Scholastic Inc. SCHOLASTIC and associated logos are trademarks and/or registered trademarks of Scholastic Inc.

Design by Steve Scott.

12   11 12 13 14 15/0

Printed in the U.S.A.   40

First printing, October 2006

Kingdoms of N'yrthghar

N

H'rathghar Mountains

Birthplace of Hoole

Bitter Sea

Firth of Fangs

Kiel Bay

Stormfast Island

H'rathghar Glacier

The Tridents

Hock

Bay of Fangs

Everwinter Sea

Elsemere Island

Ice Talons

Ice Cliff Palace

Ice Narrows

Ice Dagger

Dark Fowl Island

Kingdoms of S'yrthghar

GUARDIANS
of GA'HOOLE
THE LEGENDS

To Be a King

Contents

Prologue

"Nachtmagen!" The word hung in the air treacherous, insidious.

"Do you really think so, Coryn?" Gylfie asked. "Do you think that nachtmagen has seeped back into our world with the ember?"

The six owls peered down at the latticed iron box that contained the glowing Ember of Hoole. It was less than the cycle of one moon since Coryn had retrieved the ember from the fires of the volcano Dunmore in Beyond the Beyond to become the rightful heir to the throne of the Great Ga'Hoole Tree. Good Coryn, noble Coryn. But now the owls were shocked as Coryn spoke of this bad magic, this nachtmagen from the ancient times that threatened to destroy the owl world. Through the latticework of the box, they could see the ember's orange glow with the lick of blue in its center ringed in green. It seemed to pulsate, to breathe.

For several long nights and days the six knightly owls of the Great Ga'Hoole Tree had been reading the ancient volumes that contained the legends of Ga'Hoole. On his deathbed, Ezylryb, their beloved teacher, had instructed them to read these secret books that he had hidden away in his hollow.

"Ezylryb meant to warn us," Digger said.

"But I don't understand," Gylfie protested. She was perched on the shoulder of the Great Gray, Twilight. "We were just getting to the good part. The Great Ga'Hoole Tree and the good magic that made it grow."

Soren sighed and felt a bit of a tremor in his gizzard. "I am sure the ember brings much good. But we know that good and evil can exist side by side."

"Soren is right," Otulissa said. "Evil may cloak itself as good, and good can sometimes appear to be evil. They know each other's ways."

Coryn looked closely at Otulissa. The Spotted Owl had been his mentor in the Beyond. He trusted her greatly, but even he was surprised at how fairly she had described what he sensed were the dangers of the ember. Had King Hoole himself been aware of the perils of the ember? Had he been able to vanquish the evil? The nachtmagen? *Perhaps they would learn from this last book of the legends. He turned to Soren. "Uncle Soren, let us begin the third legend."*

Soren swept one wing over the mouse-leather cover of the ancient volume. A puff of dust swirled into the air. The tarnished gold letters seemed to shine in the glow of the coal that was set nearby. In large letters were the words: THE LEGENDS OF GA'HOOLE. And then written smaller were four words — TO BE A KING.

CHAPTER ONE

A Great Tree

It matters not who I am, only that I tell the rest of the tale . . .

Hoole flew on, a simple knight among knights. No crown, no kingly trappings. He wore only his battle claws and, from his starboard claw, hung a crude metal container. In it glowed the mysterious coal that he had retrieved from the boiling lava of the volcano Dunmore in the Beyond. The heat from that ember, though strong, was not as intense as another, more illusive power that seemed to emanate from its depths. *How odd*, Hoole thought. The ember had drained Grank of energy and caused the powerful old owl to succumb to an overwhelming lethargy of mind and body. But this was not the case for Hoole. Indeed, it was quite the opposite. He felt a new strength that almost frightened him and with it came a taste for vengeance. Vengeance for his mother's death, for his father's murder, vengeance for all the ruin and desecration that Lord Arrin and his hagsfiends had brought to a once-great kingdom. Hoole felt a deep unwelcome movement in his gizzard. Vengeance could be a distraction. And worse, vengeance was the elixir of tyrants. Creatures had been driven mad by vengeance.

On his port wing, Hoole was flanked by Grank, his mentor and foster father, and, on his starboard wing, by his two best friends: tiny Phineas, a Pygmy Owl, and Theo, a Great Horned. Behind them flew scores of owls and beneath them boiled a tempestuous sea. Through the sea's cresting waves an island broke and on that island a great tree loomed. It was the most immense tree any of the owls had ever seen. It soared out of the clouds as if to scrape the moon and fling some of its silver to make a path for the owls to follow, for a thickening fog began to swirl that obscured the sea itself. But the mist turned pearly and a luminous glow surrounded the island. Did this light come from the moon? The stars? Or the glowing ember the young king named Hoole clutched in his battle-clawed talons? Once again, the power of this ember gave Hoole pause. What were its limits? What was the reach of its light?

Hoole came fresh from the great Battle in the Beyond against the forces of Lord Arrin and his hagsfiends. Lord Arrin was the usurper of the N'yrthghar, and slayer of King H'rath, Hoole's father. Then in the Battle in the Beyond, Hoole's mother, Queen Siv, had been slain as well. Though Hoole and the H'rathian Guard had won this last battle, Hoole's gizzard twisted in the agony of loss that shadowed their triumph.

But now was not the time for mourning. A new order was to begin on this night. Now more than ever, Hoole had to reclaim his father's kingdom, oust the rebellious lords and their hideous hagsfiends. Even more important than this, he must rid the owl world of the poisonous nachtmagen that had begun to spread like some terrible disease. Until this time the cunning magic of the hagsfiends had been confined to the N'yrthghar. But for the first time hagsfiends had ventured into the S'yrthghar. Hoole dared not think what would happen if they stayed and increased. The magic they practiced was of the vilest sort.

Hoole knew the ember had great powers, but would it help him think? Would it help him lead? For that, Hoole felt he must use his firesight; there were flames to be studied. There would be new plots, ominous alliances. Lord Arrin had been beaten into retreat but not yet destroyed, and the hagsfiends were roaming the world of owls. Suddenly, Hoole's dire thoughts were interrupted by an excited shout.

"The tree! The tree!" dozens of owls hooted. The branches seemed to reach out to embrace them, and from each branch slender vines hung down, stirred by a gentle breeze. On the vines were berries the color of gold with just a touch of rose.

Grank, battle weary and thinking that indeed he had grown old, suddenly felt a tingle in his gizzard. He blinked in amazement at the sight of this huge tree. How well he remembered when they passed over the island not even a moon cycle before on their way from the N'yrthghar to the Beyond and had lighted down for a rest. The island had been barren then, with nothing but scrub and rocks.

Grank recalled how Hoole had stood apart, weeping for his mother, and how his tears had fallen on one tiny seedling just then sprouting from the barren soil. And how the tree began to grow at a miraculous rate.

How odd, he thought now as he approached the tree. *Its berries appear to be shaped like teardrops.* The old Spotted Owl blinked again to clear his eyes.

Hoole's words flooded back to Grank as they flew through the gently swaying curtains of teardrop berries. "This is a good tree. It has . . . Ga', Uncle Grank. Yes, Ga'!"

Ga' was that most elusive of all owl qualities. It literally meant "great spirit"; a spirit that somehow did not contain only all that is noble but all that is humble, as well.

*   *   *

Hoole had been right in bringing them back to this tree and not directly to the N'yrthghar. It was not yet time to go north. *All in due course ... all in due course,* thought Grank.

Suddenly, there was a great din in Grank's ear slits, a surging up of hoots and chimes, of hoo-hoos, woo-woos, and whoops. Every species of owl had its own particular way of hooting, but they were all crying out the same words: "The Great Ga'Hoole Tree! The Great Ga'Hoole Tree!"

The young king swiveled his head and blinked in confusion at his mentor. "What is this?"

Grank churred softly and replied, "They have named the tree Hoole."

"But —" Hoole started to say.

"Yes, Great Spirit of Hoole. It is named for you, Hoole, and rightfully so."

CHAPTER TWO

Just Plain Hoole?

Outside the Great Ga'Hoole tree, a late summer storm raged and lightning peeled back the sky. But inside the tree, which still continued to grow but more slowly, all was dry and cozy. Even with the loudest claps of thunder, the immense tree hardly shuddered. Hoole was in the loveliest hollow he could ever imagine, gazing at the ember glowing through the piercings in a small metal container. Grank flew into the hollow.

"Ah, a lovely new box, Your Grace."

Hoole looked up at his mentor in dismay. "Not you, too!"

"Me, too, what, Your Majesty?"

"We've been here barely three nights, and everywhere I turn it's 'Your Grace,' 'Your Highness,' 'Your Majesty.' I can't stand it. If you start, too, Uncle Grank, I'll feel I have lost my oldest friend."

"You must understand, Hoole, these titles are a form

of respect. It is important that respect be maintained if you are to lead."

"But it is action and words that earns one respect, isn't it?"

"Yes, a title is worthless without the gallgrot to back it up. But it is protocol, after all."

This word confused Hoole. He guessed it had to do with how a king's or queen's retinue paid homage to their monarch; very much about ritual and manners. It sounded incredibly boring to Hoole, and very restrictive.

Grank, for his part, had to remind himself continually that Hoole was a different kind of monarch. He had been raised about as far as one could be from the elaborate rituals of court behavior. So why bog him down with rigid procedures and detailed codes of manners and ritual?

Grank looked at the new container for the ember. "The new box is lovely. Very different shape — not square as before. Almost a . . ." Grank hesitated. He had been about to say "teardrop," but instead said "berry."

"Yes," Hoole whispered. "Theo took the old one and reshaped it." Hoole also resisted saying the word "teardrop." Theo had not known about Hoole's tears. The Great Horned blacksmith had merely thought the shape of the berries lovely.

"You know, they say the berries taste like what some

creatures call milk," Grank added. "Some owls call them milkberries now," Grank said.

"Oh, really?" *Thank Glaux they're not Hoole berries or some such nonsense!* Hoole thought.

"Well," Grank said, "Theo has done wonders with his forge. So lucky he found that cave. He's got his fires going. And, he has come around to making battle claws."

"I know it must have been a hard decision, Theo being a gizzard-resister and all," Hoole said.

"It was the battle that changed him," Grank offered. "And, of course, the idea of hagsfiends and nachtmagen let loose in the world." He paused. "Well, I think I shall turn in for the day, Your —" He stopped himself. "Hoole, I'll tell you what: I'll make a deal with you. I'll not call you Your Grace or any of those titles that you seem to loathe if you'll not call me Uncle."

"You don't like being called Uncle?" Hoole blinked in surprise.

Grank's yellow eyes softened. "I love it. It stirs my gizzard like no other word, I think. But if you are to be king, it does not suit to call your chief advisor Uncle."

"I see," Hoole replied. "All right, Grank. You shall be Grank and I shall be just plain Hoole."

Hardly, Grank thought as he left the hollow. *Hardly "just plain Hoole"!*

CHAPTER THREE

Meditations on an Ember

Hoole resumed his study of the ember in the iron teardrop. "I am king because of you, ember," he whispered. It startled him that he had addressed the ember as if it were a living creature. But in a curious way it felt right. The ember was said to have great powers. He had heard in great detail from the wolf Fengo that its powers nearly overcame Grank when he first retrieved it years ago. Hoole thought about magic and why even good magic might not truly be the way to rule. It was disturbing to him that some of the owls of the tree were thinking of him as not only a king but a mage. He disliked the title "mage" even more than that of "king."

"How dangerous you can be!" he spoke in that same hushed voice to the ember. It seemed to pulse and the blue glow at its center darkened. "So many want you. Would kill for you. So many think that your magic will grant them all powers, perhaps even immortality, eh?" The ember gave a little hiss and a bit of fiery spittle escaped the iron teardrop. *So,* thought Hoole, *this ember forces us to balance on a blade's edge between a kingship and tyranny, between principles of justice and magic.* "Somehow I must make all owls of the Great Tree understand this danger."

The lovely voice of the Snow Rose, the gadfeather who had fought with them in the Beyond, began to filter through the tree. She had taken to singing ballads toward First Light as the owls nestled in for the day.

Where go the stars,
where goes the dark,
the night so black and clear?
Worry not, worry not,
night will come again soon.
Dark, dark, fold me in your wings.
Dark, dark, let my gizzard sing.
But now is the time for light —
let it come, let it come.
Bring the sun so bright,
then the shadows beyond the noon
grow long as day grows old.
Worry not, my owls,
the dark will wait for you.
Worry not, the night steals away the day.
Worry not, twilight turns to gray.

Here comes the night,
here comes the night.

Hoole had been so glad that the Snow Rose had decided to stay at least temporarily. But Grank had warned him that gadfeathers rarely remained in any place for long. "Remember, Hoole, she's already tried being a Glauxian Sister. And she left that after a very short time. Once a gadfeather, always a gadfeather," Grank had cautioned.

Hoole thought about this now. For the past three nights she had sung to them at daybreak. Daybreak could be a hard time for owls. The night was gone and everything seemed too bright. But she had made it a more comfortable, friendlier time. *Perhaps that was it!* Hoole suddenly realized a thing of great importance. The Snow Rose might stay because she had a unique role to play here. If each owl thought he or she was special and vital to the tree, it would not only make them loyal but also perhaps distract them from notions of magic and mages. More than that, it could make this tree truly great if each owl used their special talents. The Snow Rose was much more than a gadfeather. She was an artist and a warrior. Just as Theo was much more than a blacksmith who forged weapons. He must learn to make many useful things beyond battle claws and containers for embers. Hoole looked at the iron teardrop now.

Suppose, thought Hoole, *Theo might be able to make many similar containers, and we could put coals in them to light the many hollows in the tree.* If certain hollows were always illuminated, learning could go on all the time.

And Grank himself was a collier. He must teach others if the skill was not to be lost eventually. There were so many things to be taught, to be learned. The Great Ga'Hoole Tree could become great beyond its mere size. It would be the beginning of a new era that would be Glaux blessed and free of magic or nachtmagen. *Now how to explain all of this to the parliament?*

He poked his beak out of the hollow and summoned a young lieutenant from the Ice Regiment of H'rath, who had been perched as a lookout.

"Yes, Your Majesty?" The Barn Owl swept down from his high perch.

"No sign of Joss?" Hoole asked.

"No sign, Your Majesty."

"Thank you, Cuthmore. Alert me at the first sign of him."

"Certainly, Your Majesty."

This was deeply troubling. Joss was their most reliable messenger. He had served Hoole's father, King H'rath, and had kept Grank himself informed during Grank's long absences from his court. They were dependent on Joss, a tough Whiskered Screech, for any and all news from the Northern Kingdoms. It was urgent that they know how much damage Lord Arrin had sustained. Was he rebuilding his army? And what about the hagsfiends? Had any been killed? Hoole was furious with himself that he had not thought to dispatch Joss first to the Southern Kingdoms to see if any were lingering there. Hagsfiends in the S'yrthghar would prove disastrous. *Why did I not do this?* Hoole demanded of himself for what felt like the tenth time.

I must learn to think like a commander, to think like a king. No, Hoole corrected himself. *I must learn to* be *a king.*

CHAPTER FOUR

To Be a Guardian

It was a strange word, "parliament." Hoole had never heard it before. But Grank had explained to him that a parliament was a group of owls that gather together for discussion and decision making. Hoole had decided that a hollow near the base of the tree was the perfect place for the parliament.

So eleven owls, including Hoole, now perched in a half circle of niches and notches that were scattered around the walls of a hollow in the great tree. Hoole was in the center. He swiveled his head to one side and then the other, taking in each owl. Some, like Phineas, Theo, and Grank, were his old friends. Some he had only recently met. They had been rallied from the remnants of the old H'rathian Guard to fight in the Beyond. He studied these new ones now. There was Lord Rathnik, one of his father's closest advisors, who had led the Ice Regiment of H'rath in the battle and fought brilliantly. The officers of the Ice

Regiment had all been knights, and it was Lord Rathnik who had knighted Hoole.

For Hoole, this conferring of knighthood was more important than being anointed as king. He had already decided that he would wear no crown. And if Hoole had his way, the tree would not be called the Great Ga'Hoole Tree, but simply the great tree.

To one side of Hoole, Grank perched. Next to him was Theo, then Phineas. On the other side of Hoole was Lord Rathnik, and beside Lord Rathnik, Sir Garthnore, a Snowy Owl, and his mate, Lady Helling; a Northern Hawk Owl, Sir Tobyfyor (or Toby); Lord Vladkyn, who was a Screech; Sir Bors, a Barn Owl; and finally, a Spotted Owl named Strix Strumajen.

Hoole blinked at the assembled group. He knew what they were thinking: *Where is the ember?* This, after all, was the symbol of his power. The owls, perched in their niches, tried not to appear anxious, but there was an undeniable agitation in the parliament hollow as the birds discreetly swiveled their heads, searching for the ember.

Finally, Sir Garthnore nervously clacked his beak and began, "Er . . . Your Grace, is something amiss with the ember?"

"No, no, it is safely tucked away," Hoole said. "I have set two guards upon it."

"Is that wise, Your Grace?" asked Lord Vladkyn.

"Why would it be unwise, Lord Vladkyn? Are you fearful someone might steal it?"

"No, Your Grace. But we have sworn allegiance to you because you are the one who retrieved the ember." A murmur of assent rippled through the parliament as the owls turned to one another and nodded in agreement. "It seems only fitting."

"Why?" Hoole asked.

The Lord Rathnik spoke. "We wish to invest Your Majesty with absolute power. That is what we thought was the point of this gathering. It seems only fitting, therefore, to elevate you — you who hold the ember."

Grank was watching Hoole carefully. *This would be the test,* Grank thought.

"This is difficult to explain," Hoole began, "but I have come to you today to tell you that I do not want absolute power." There was a great stirring and grumbling in the hollow. "Quiet! Quiet!" Hoole seized a stick of wood and rapped on the hollow's walls. "Listen to me. The time has come for a new order. I shall be your king. But you cannot simply hand over power. True, part of my power comes from the ember. But another part does not."

"Your Highness, from whence does it come?" Sir Garthnore bellowed in the great booming tones of a Snowy.

A surge of voices now called out: "From where does this power come, if not the ember?" "Tell us, sir."

"Let him speak!" It was Strix Strumajen. Hoole had noticed that she had not joined in the hue and cry with the others but had remained quite still, with her eyes settled on him.

"The ember does have powers," Hoole answered, "and should it fall into the wrong talons, it would be disastrous. I shall do all I can to prevent that. But the powers of the ember come from magen — magic. Magic is not a justifiable reason for power."

"Magic is not reason, Your Grace. So why question it with reason?" Lady Helling asked. There was a murmur of approval that passed through the hollow.

"I do not question magic. But I question your willingness to let it, through the ember, rule over you. You must think of power as a tree. The roots of a tree are what anchor it to the earth and let it soar, like this tree, into the sky. They are the reasons a tree grows. And I tell you now that the roots of power for *us* who live in this great tree must be the ideals of goodness, equality, and nobility. I have chosen to have our parliamentary hollow here, near the roots of the tree, as a constant reminder of the true sources of power. Do not give me power that I have not earned. Do not make me an absolute ruler. I am your king, but we must come together as equals to discuss and decide our course. It is not birth or magic that makes one noble. We are only as noble as our actions prove us to be. I hope to rid the owl world not just of nachtmagen, but of all magen — both good and bad. I am an owl first, a king second, but never a mage. Never."

The owls had quieted. Grank looked at the young king with wonder and thought, *I am in the presence of great Ga'*.

"Now, let me tell you my plan. . . ." And so Hoole began to explain his vision to the knights of the great tree. "When I was very young on that island in the Bitter Sea, Grank told me stories of owls in the early part of my grandfather King H'rathmore's reign, tales of owls who came together for sport to display their skills and learn in small groups called chaws. So, what I propose is that we divide the members of the tree into different chaws that will come together to learn new things."

"New things? What new things?" Sir Bors asked.

"We have many great talents here among us. Sir Bors, I have heard that you understand how the stars move across the night sky, and that your knowledge is far beyond the navigational abilities of most owls. Could you not teach this better way of navigating?"

"S'pose I could. . . . Yes, s'pose I could, Your Grace."

"And Strix Strumajen, I heard that you are particularly sensitive, like many Spotted Owls, to changes in the weight of air, and that you can interpret these changes in pressure to guess what weather might be coming in."

"It is not a guess, sir. It is a type of reasoning that has proven very accurate for forecasting and interpreting weather patterns."

"Could you not lead a chaw that would train other owls to interpret the weather?"

"Well, yes, Your Grace, I could. I would be most happy to. But should it be just Spotted Owls?"

"I think not. I think any owl should be able to learn about this if he or she is truly interested. We shouldn't let our kind, how we were born, limit us."

There was real excitement in the hollow now as the young king shared his vision for the new things owls would be learning. Grank would lead a colliering chaw, and Theo would teach owls the secrets of shaping metal. Best of all, none of this was magic. None of it depended on anything but an individual owl's own skills and effort.

The meeting of the parliament was drawing to a close. It was time for Hoole's last stroke, his finishing touch to the new order. "We have come together as knights in battle, and we shall come together again in battle to vanquish the hagsfiends and the legions of Lord Arrin, the usurper. But now, here, we have come together in a new way." Hoole paused and regarded each of the ten other members of the parliament. "You have already taken your oaths as knights and now I am going to ask you to take yet another oath." There was a look of keen expectation in the eyes of the owls. *What kind of oath would this be?* they wondered.

"Fear not," Hoole said. "We shall guard the ember ferociously, but I have told you that the ember is but one source of power. The deeper and stronger power is the one we have established here today. It, too, must be guarded and tended like the roots of a tree that burgeons from the earth and soars into the sky. And those roots are nurtured by goodness, equality, and nobility. We must become the Guardians of Ga'Hoole. I am asking you to take this oath along with me."

There was a great stillness in the hollow. And then ten voices began to repeat the words their young king spoke: "I am a Guardian of Ga'Hoole. From this night on, I dedicate my life to the protection of owlkind. I shall not swerve in my duty. I shall support my brother and sister Guardians in times of battle, as well as in times of peace. I am the eyes in the night, the silence within the wind. I am the talons through the fire, the shield that guards the innocent. I shall seek to wear no crown, nor win any glory. And all these things I do swear upon my honor as a Guardian of Ga'Hoole until my days on this earth cease to be. This be my vow. This be my life. By Glaux, I do swear."

CHAPTER FIVE

The Hagsfiend of the Ice Narrows

Deep in a cave of the Ice Narrows, that channel of water connecting the Southern and the Northern Waters, the hagsfiend Ygryk watched as an egg trembled. She was not alone. Another, a Great Horned Owl named Pleek, stood behind his mate. Some might call their union — hagsfiend and owl — unholy, but in their own peculiar way, they did love each other. And yet they could not have chicks, for unions such as theirs were barren. But Ygryk, despite her haggish ways, had an obsession to mother. She was desperate for a chick and so driven that she dared fly over open water, which could prove fatal to hagsfiends because their feathers lacked the natural oils of many birds. If their crowlike black feathers came in contact with salt water, they became sodden and their weight dragged them down into the sea. But despite this hazard, she and Pleek had come to live in the Ice Narrows with Kreeth, an immensely powerful hagsfiend who dared to live above the open water of the Ice Narrows. Her reason for this, she stated simply: "Water is my enemy. Keep your friends close, and your enemies closer."

Kreeth had spent a lifetime in her cave above the churning waters of the Narrows, studying to divine a charm that would render her and all hagsfiends immune to the ravages of seawater. So far, she had not succeeded. Nonetheless, she had developed powerful charms and could claim a nachtmagen unequaled among hagsfiends. But she had always worked alone. A recluse, she had vowed never to mate, nor would she become a tool for the likes of Lord Arrin, to fight his stupid battles for a stupid throne and a crown of ice. Just as Ygryk had a peculiar and un-haggish urge to mother, Kreeth herself possessed an odd and un-haggish sense of honor. It was not that she was against war. Kreeth entertained no reservations about killing. She was opposed to war because she thought it was stupid, and dependent on brute force and coarse strategies rather than on charms and spells. And there were very few charms or spells, save for the fyngrot, that worked on a battlefield.

At this moment in her ice hollow, Kreeth tried not to

listen as Pleek went on about the defeat of Lord Arrin's forces in the Beyond by young King Hoole. Once again, Ygryk sighed with regret. She had so desperately wanted Hoole for her own chick. She and Pleek had tried to capture him, and nearly had him with a special fyngrot spell that Kreeth had given her. But they had been attacked at the last minute, their one chance lost. Both she and Pleek had been gravely wounded.

"Stop sighing, Ygryk. What's done is done. You keep this sighing up and you're never going to get your half-hags back. They don't incubate well if their host has her feathers in a twist over something," Kreeth scolded. Half-hags were the minuscule, poisonous creatures who lived in the small gaps and narrow slotted spaces between the feathers of hagsfiends. In battle, they could dart out with their toxic load and attack. But perhaps the best service that half-hags could perform, with the proper nurturing and training, was that of tracking.

"Now pull yourself together, Ygryk," Kreeth cautioned, "I have something coming here that, well — how should I put it — might fulfill your motherly desires. Although why anyone would want to mother anything is beyond me. Creating creatures in one's own image is completely boring in my way of thinking. I only create new life to study it. To see the possibilities."

Pleek looked around the cave nervously as Kreeth spoke. On the walls, suspended from ice hooks, were the heads of owls killed in battle. It was the practice of the warrior hagsfiends to cut off the heads of their victims, impale them on the tips of their ice swords, and then fly off with them triumphantly from the battlefield. Kreeth offered handsome rewards for several heads. She also collected the ashes of those burned in final ceremonies. But final ceremonies were a ritual of the S'yrthghar, where owls knew how to handle fire. In the north, these ashes were hard to come by. Kreeth craved them for their extremely powerful effect in her haggish recipes.

With her spells and foul ingredients, she had created some truly monstrous forms of birdlife. Some of their shriveled carcasses hung on the ice cave walls, like trophies of creations gone wrong, along with the neatly dried gizzards and strings of withered eyeballs of birds she had murdered. But one of her creations was alive. Looking at it caused alarm in Pleek's own gizzard, or what was left of his gizzard after his union with Ygryk. As soon as an owl begins to consort with hagsfiends, a slow deterioration would set in on that once noble organ. So the sad remnants of Pleek's gizzard quivered slightly at the sight of Kreeth's puffowl, a cross between a puffin and a Snowy Owl. It was the vilest thing Pleek had ever seen. It waddled around with the pure white face of a Snowy disfigured by the garish markings and the big, fat, blunt beak of a puffin.

Kreeth had originally felt that it was best to use transformational charms and spells on a hatchling or very young bird and not try to do anything with the egg itself. But she had recently changed her thoughts about this, or rather her "philosophy," as she liked to say. For Kreeth preferred to think of herself not merely as a practitioner of nachtmagen, but a scientist and a philosopher, as well.

"Pleek, Ygryk!" Kreeth called. "Its egg tooth is pecking out!"

The egg that was now about to hatch was that of a Great Horned she had stolen, which she had then "touched" with a crow feather. Touched in this case did not literally mean touching, but involved an incantation during what she called the primary spell phase.

Excitement coursed through the ice cave. Ygryk and Pleek pressed closer. One thought gripped them both. *This could be ours! A chick at last!* Kreeth heard a shuffling from a dim corner of the cave and swiveled her head quickly toward the puffowl. "Get away from those hearts. I'm marinating them. Get out of here."

"Yes, Mummy!" the puffowl said, and waddled away in dejection.

"How many times do I have to tell you? Don't call me Mummy! I'm not your frinkin' mummy! You're my experiment."

Then she turned to Pleek. "It should be hatching any second."

There was a big cracking sound, then a blob of a tiny bird flopped out. "What is it?" Pleek whispered.

Kreeth cackled. "We'll just have to wait and see. You ordered a Great Horned, didn't you?

"Yes, but is it?"

"Could be this. Could be that," Kreeth replied slyly.

"It does look like an owl, Pleek," Ygryk said. "Bulgy eyes." She and Pleek were bending over the little creature.

"Are you disappointed, dear? Did you want it to be more haggish?"

"No, no, Pleek. All I want is a nice little chick."

What they got was indeed a chick. Whether she would be a nice little chick was doubtful. But the real question was: What species did she belong to? All chicks look very similar at the time of hatching. Nearly bald, their eye color murky, the newly hatched creatures are shapeless and fairly indistinguishable. But when they begin to fledge and their eye color becomes clearer, they bear all the features of their species.

*   *   *

For several days after hatching, it did appear to Pleek that the chick had all the first signs of being a Great Horned like Pleek. Her eyes were becoming the bright yellow of a Great Horned. It did make Pleek nervous, though, how Kreeth seemed more interested in observing himself and Ygryk than the chick. There was a cunning about Kreeth that he found very unsettling and every time he would say something about how it looked as if the chick were indeed turning out to be a Great Horned Owl, he swore he could hear Kreeth snort under her breath. It was right after the chick had lost her downy fluff and fledged her first feathers, which looked so much like Great Horned plumage, that something odd occurred.

Pleek and Ygryk were returning from a short hunting flight and had just flown into the ice cave to deposit their prey.

"How's our little one?" Pleek boomed. Then he heard a sharp cry from Ygryk.

"What happened? My baby!"

"Has she been hurt? Is she dead?" Pleek spun his head toward Kreeth. "What have you done, you crone?"

"Nothing," she cackled, "except to create a masterpiece."

"Pleek, look at her!" Ygryk gasped.

He lofted himself over to where the chick was poking around for some ice worms. The little chick looked up at her da and blinked. Pleek felt his withered gizzard give a lurch. He was looking into the black eyes of a female Barn Owl, but her body had the coloration of a Great Horned. "Wh— wh— what happened? How could this be?" And then her face started to lose the tawny feathers of a Great Horned and to turn white. Even her shape seemed to lengthen a bit and widen slightly at the top so that it appeared more like that of a Barn Owl. "A Barn Owl! I never!" Pleek gasped in disbelief.

"You never, is right!" Kreeth's words bit the air. "I did this. And I shall name her Lutta. Lutta is my masterpiece. She is everything. And nothing."

"What do you mean?" Ygryk cried. "All we wanted was one little chick that looked like one of us, or maybe both. What have you done? She'll belong to neither of us."

"That is your decision, my dear," Kreeth replied. "But look at her. Look at what I have created." Now the white face of the Barn Owl was turning the deep glistening black of a crow. The eyes were becoming beady crow's eyes.

Within a single day, Lutta went through a half dozen transformations. For a few hours she was a crow. Then she slid almost imperceptibly into being a Barred Owl. Next a Snowy. The most spectacular shift was when, within the space of seconds, she would go from the total blackness of a crow to the pure whiteness of a Snowy. But perhaps her best transformation was when she changed into a Spotted Owl.

Lutta seemed cheerful enough, and Pleek and Ygryk were pleased, they guessed, that she called them Mum and Da, but they had a difficult time relating to this chick that Kreeth called a changeling.

"It's genius what I have done!" Kreeth exclaimed several times a day and into the night. And despite all her protestations about not wanting to be a mother, she seemed genuinely fond of Lutta in an almost maternal sense.

"But all this changing — it's not natural," Pleek protested in the gentlest way.

Kreeth blinked her beady little eyes. "You think either one of you is natural? Who needs natural? Lutta is interesting. She's a fascinating phenomenon."

"Yes, yes, of course." Pleek and Ygryk nodded. Silently, they reminded themselves that they had a unique and wonderful chick. But each one silently thought, *We didn't want a phenomenon, we just wanted a chick! Something we can call our own.* Still, they tried to appreciate this wondrous chick. To learn her ways. To come to love her and delight in her.

And for a while, it worked. Pleek and Ygryk told themselves that underneath the plumy whiteness of a Snowy Owl or the speckled splendor of a Spotted Owl or the silvery mist featheration of a Great Gray, she was still their little Lutta. Although it was especially upsetting to Pleek when he had brought her a plump little ice mouse for her first Meat-on-Bones ceremony that Lutta changed species a half-dozen times during the ritual. She started off as a Great Horned, then slid into the dark sleekness of hagsfiend. Pleek and Ygryk both churred at this, for they took it as an homage to themselves. "So respectful!" Ygryk murmured. And it would have been if it had ended there. But it did not. A moment later, Lutta had become a Pygmy Owl, of all things, and dwindled to such a tiny size that she could hardly get the plump thigh of the ice mouse down her gullet.

"Great Glaux, why would she do a thing like that?" Pleek fumed. Lutta blinked at him. "Why are you calling me she, Da, and not Lutta?" Pleek didn't answer.

"Mum, why's he calling me she? I'm your chick. It's like you don't know me."

"We find it . . . hard sometimes, dear," Ygryk stammered as she watched the Pygmy swell into a Barn Owl, then peered into the shining dark eyes that gleamed black as river stones in that stark white face. "It is you in there, isn't it?" she asked in a tremulous voice.

From a corner in the ice hollow, Kreeth cast a sly glance.

Pleek and Ygryk were becoming less and less sure of Lutta. When out on their hunting flights, they would discuss their peculiar owlet.

"I just don't know what to make of it, Pleek."

"I know what you mean, my dear. I suppose we'll have to teach her to fly," Pleek said wearily. "As you say, it's hard to know how to feel."

Any child, bird or otherwise, can sense their parents' doubt, and Lutta was no exception. At first it made her angry, but then she began to feel rather indifferent. What did she care what they thought? Kreeth was always good to her. Kreeth liked her the way she was — whatever that was. She began to dread when Pleek and Ygryk returned from their hunting trips. They always seemed to be whispering about her. She could sense it just before they entered the cave. And then they would either stare at her and not say anything or turn their heads as if it hurt them to look at her. But Kreeth was the opposite. She seemed to delight in all of Lutta's transformations.

On this particular night, her parents had just returned

and she was perched on her ice ledge as a crow, which she thought Ygryk would like, but Ygryk just got this hard look in her eye. *By the demons of smee holes,* thought Lutta, using a favorite curse of Kreeth's, *why is my haggish, so-called mother staring at me like this?* "Look!" She blurted out. "I can't help what I am and what I am not." Kreeth craftily observed all this from a corner in the cave.

"I suppose that is so," was all that Ygryk said. And Pleek went silently to his ice perch without even greeting Lutta.

At noon the following day, as Kreeth and Lutta slept, Pleek and Ygryk left. They abandoned their longed-for chick to the hagsfiend who had divined her.

CHAPTER SIX
The Education of Lutta

The inside of the ice cave danced with the light of the stars outside. They were called frost stars because their images were reflected perfectly on the ice walls as they rose in the night.

Lutta blinked. "I overslept." She swiveled her head, which, at this time, had taken the form and featheration of a Barn Owl. Her eyes, like black mirrors, reflected the frost stars. Even Kreeth was struck by her beauty. "They're gone, aren't they?" She turned to the hagsfiend, who nodded. "And tonight was to be my First Flight. Here I am, fully fledged at last. Figures!" She spat out the word with contempt.

"Don't you worry, dearie. I can teach you better than they ever could." Kreeth watched her. The white face was beginning to turn tawny. Yellow suffused the black eyes. Another one of Lutta's myriad transformations was beginning. It was in response to her rejection. On some level, she was trying to become what her foster parents had wanted. It was triggered by the sickening feelings of shame and abandonment.

Kreeth knew that her own task was to raise this extraordinary young creature. And Kreeth had big plans for her. Let the others fight their wars in the Northern and the Southern Kingdoms. Let them fight over territory and ice thrones and ice crowns. A new dynasty was beginning right here in this cave in the Ice Narrows. A dynasty born of the darkest and most impenetrable of charms — and Lutta would be its beginning.

But first, Kreeth must instruct her how to control her changes. She probably had no inkling that she herself could influence the timing of the change or the species she changed into. "Lutta, I love you for what you are and what you are not." Kreeth spoke very slowly. She fixed her dark eyes on the fading black orbs of Lutta. "What you are and are not is the sum of your whole." Indeed, the transformation was slowing down. The yellow of the Great Horned's eyes seemed to dim as the black of the Barn Owl's flooded back and the face feathered white.

It might have seemed to Lutta that Kreeth spoke in riddles. But she did feel something happening. The transformation slowed. She felt a sense of peace within her for the first time. She looked down. Her breast was white with a few light speckles. Her wings were tan with dashes of white. Kreeth was regarding her with great interest. *She is understanding for the first time these differences. This is good. This is very good.*

"It stopped," Lutta gasped in wonder.

"You stopped it."

"How? How did I do it?"

"By learning who you are, by being keenly aware of the differences. What did you feel first in your face?"

"I felt it lengthening and narrowing toward the bottom. The top is wider than the bottom."

"Exactly. And what else?"

"The whiteness of my face. I felt that. I don't know how you can feel color, but I did."

"You sensed the light-reflecting qualities of white. That is all."

"And I could hear better, too!"

"Yes, of course. You see, my dear, if you concentrate on the key elements that make a particular owl, you can control these changes. You can summon them or dismiss them at will. You *shall* control them. They *shall not* control you. This makes you important."

"It does?" she asked.

She is completely unsuspecting. This will make it even more fun for me! Kreeth thought. "Lutta, you have power — great power. They talk of the Ember of Hoole, but you have a power to match that of the ember and that of the king who possesses it."

"What can I do with the power?"

"Rule, my dear. You can become the first monarch of a new dynasty."

A poisonous look infused Lutta's black Barn Owl eyes. She felt a minute stirring in her primary feathers.

Demons of smee! Kreeth thought. *Her first hagsfiends are hatching! She is too good to be true! Hagsfiends roosting in the feathers of a Barn Owl! Delightful! And she hasn't even learned how to fly yet!*

"Can I punish my parents? Make Pleek and Ygryk suffer?"

Oh, thought Kreeth, *I've made a good one here.* Some, Kreeth realized, might think it was a waste of energy to seek such petty revenge. Pleek and Ygryk hardly seemed worth it. Still, vengeance had its uses. Vengeance could feed the fire that burned within this creature. Vengeance was like a flint stone on which Lutta might sharpen her talons.

"Of course, dear. But believe me, there are greater prey than those two. Right now we must get to the business of flying. How would you like to learn to fly? As a Barn Owl? A Snowy? Northern Hawk Owl? Great Gray?"

"Great Gray," Lutta replied.

"Nice choice. Lovely fliers, with all that fluffy plumage. Now begin to concentrate on what you have experienced so far during one of your transformations into a Great Gray."

The transformations were sometimes so fleeting that it was difficult for Lutta to remember everything and she hesitated.

"Start with the head, Lutta. Always start with the head," Kreeth counseled. Lutta snapped her beak shut and began to feel the bottom of her face expand. Her head was becoming larger and rounder. Her face expanded to nearly twice its size. Her plumage grew denser and silvery.

"Come with me, dearie. Our flight lessons begin!"

CHAPTER SEVEN

Strix Strumajen Yearning

A cry was heard. "He's sighted! Joss is sighted!"

Then Cuthbert, commander of the second watch, flew into Hoole's hollow. "Begging your pardon, Your Grace, but we done caught a glimpse of him in the dawn. It's Joss, all right. He's back!" Hoole was instantly alert. "So sorry to interrupt your sleep, what with tween time hardly passed."

"Don't go apologizing, Commander. This couldn't have happened soon enough."

Within seconds, Hoole was at the top of the great tree, peering into the rose-colored dawn. "Bless my gizzard and thank Glaux, he's back." Before anyone could blink, Hoole launched himself onto a rising thermal and flew out to greet the faithful messenger, the Whiskered Screech, Joss.

"Let him catch his breath, lad, let him catch his breath," Grank called from below.

"No need, sir," Joss replied. "There is much to tell and no time to be wasted."

39

"Sorry, sorry," Hoole apologized. "Here, come to the hollow and rest first."

"May I begin, sir?" Joss asked as he settled onto a perch in Hoole's hollow.

"Please. What is the news?"

"You did a right good deal of damage to Lord Arrin, no doubt about it, Your Majesty."

Hoole interrupted. "Joss, please do not call me Your Majesty. It's just the three of us here." Hoole nodded at Grank.

"Oh, certainly . . . well . . . sir, many have broken with Lord Arrin. Lost faith, I guess you'd say. But, at the same time, new alliances are being formed. Of that you can be sure."

"Yes, I feared that. There was always that possibility. But so soon?"

"Apparently."

"Do you know the nature of these alliances?"

"Well, we know for sure that Ullryck has deserted."

"Ullryck! Ullryck was Lord Arrin's best assassin, wasn't she, Grank?" Hoole turned to look at his counselor.

"Indeed," Grank replied gravely.

"It's rumored that she has started her own division of hagsfiends."

"Just hagsfiends? Nothing else?" Hoole asked.

"Just hagsfiends," Joss replied.

Hoole and Grank exchanged looks and blinked. This had always been their worst fear. An army of just hagsfiends. And then they both had the same unspoken thought. Though they were both flame readers, the fires had rarely rendered clear images of hagsfiends. It was as if the hagsfiends' magic in some way inhibited the clarity of the flames. Images became garbled, almost nonsensical, and certainly not trustworthy. But, Hoole wondered, was the answer to turn to the magic of the ember? Was this when he must fight magic with magic? He did not like the notion.

"Tell us more," Grank urged.

"There are rumors of a young upstart — an owl, not a hagsfiend — from someplace far north of the Firth of Fangs, but no one is quite sure who he is. If he has an alliance with hagsfiends, it is not known at this time." Joss paused. "And finally, I fear that I have some troubling news for Strix Strumajen."

"Oh, dear!" Grank groaned deeply. "What is it?"

"Her daughter, Emerilla, has been lost in a skirmish over the Ice Fangs."

"Lost, you say?" Grank blinked at Joss. "But not killed?"

"Not as far as we know, sir. There were a great number of hagsfiends in the battle and if they had killed her,

41

well, you know . . ." Nothing further needed to be said, for they all knew of the ghoulish practices of hagsfiends in battle.

"Call her mother here immediately," Hoole said.

As soon as Strix Strumajen entered the hollow and spied Joss, she seemed to know. Her feathers flattened and she wilfed to nearly half her size. "She's dead. My dear Emerilla is dead."

"Not dead, milady," Joss said softly. "Missing . . . for now."

"There was no . . . no . . . head?" she asked quietly.

Hoole's gizzard clenched. How hard it must be for this owl to suddenly refer to her daughter as simply a head.

"No, ma'am. No head."

Strix Strumajen recovered a bit. Her feathers plumped up slightly. She turned to Hoole. "She is a dear young owl, and you know, Your Grace, Emerilla's gift for interpreting weather was —" she hesitated "— is even greater than mine. She would be such an addition to the tree."

Hoole made a short flight from one perch to another in his hollow. Above this perch was a somewhat crude map that one of the members of the H'rathian Guard had brought with him from the N'yrthghar. "The Ice Fangs, I don't see it here."

"It's off the Bay of Fangs. It isn't on this map. It was a short but brutal battle that took place there," Joss said.

Strix Strumajen shook her head. "She wanted to go into battle so badly. I felt she was too young. But then you, Hoole, are about the same age as she. Siv and I laid our eggs during the same moon cycle. Emerilla was determined to fight, after her father was killed over the Ice Dagger. We all thought that she was too small to manage one of the long scimitars. But, by Glaux, if she didn't go harvest herself a small blade from the issen vingtygg. It took courage to use, for it required close fighting. She was so quick with it. So bold!" Strix Strumajen's dark amber eyes filled with tears.

Hoole dropped his beak and ran it through the feathers on his chest. He was thinking very hard and coming to the edge of an important idea. He looked up and blinked at the three owls. "I don't want us to lose another owl to these hagsfiends and tyrants. We must act now. If we do not take the battle to them, they will bring the battle to us, to the tree."

"Whoever chooses the battlefield wins the battle," Grank said in a low, gravelly voice.

"Precisely!" Hoole nodded. "But I am choosing more than one battlefield."

"More than one, sir?" Grank blinked. "Is that wise?"

"Well, you see . . ." Hoole swiveled his head slowly.

"Not all of them will appear to be battlefields. Not all of them will require the same amount of power or resources, but they will be crucial to our ultimate victory."

"I don't follow, sir," said Joss.

"Let me explain." Hoole pointed to the map of the N'yrthghar and lifted it with his talons to reveal another equally crude map of the S'yrthghar. "We must deal with three realms essentially — that of the N'yrthghar, the S'yrthghar, and our own realm here at the great tree. In one realm, we must fight," he said, pointing to the spot where the great palace of the H'rathghar glacier rose out of the N'yrthghar ice fields. "In another, we must train." He tapped the tiny island in the vast sea of the Southern Kingdoms. "And here" — he swept his four talons lightly across the great expanse of the continent of the Southern Kingdoms, including that westernmost region known as Beyond the Beyond — "we must find out who our friends are, and if there are hagsfiends anywhere."

Hoole flew to the Spotted Owl's side and tapped her shoulder gently with his wing tip and even preened her back feathers a bit with his beak. "Strix Strumajen, your knowledge of weather is invaluable, but you also have great skill with a variety of weapons. I saw you practicing with battle claws the other evening. You were superb. You will be a formidable threat on this battlefield." Once more, he indicated the place on the map where his ancestral palace on the H'rathghar glacier stood. "I want you to train a new company of owls with the short blade. Teach them everything you know."

"It will be an honor, Your Grace."

"Joss, your job is to set up a slipgizzling system in the N'yrthghar. You have been both messenger and spy for years now. It is too much for one owl. We need more information. Find noncombat owls, even gizzard-resisters, who are ready and willing to give it to us."

"Yes, Your Majesty. That will be most helpful."

Hoole tapped his head with a single talon. "And why not use polar bears as slipgizzles, too?" Hoole blinked at his own question.

"A wonderful idea!" Joss exclaimed. "I know several."

"With your contacts up there, Joss, we'll at least have a chance of keeping track of the new alliances."

"If I may offer a suggestion, Your Grace?" Strix Strumajen stepped forward.

"Certainly, ma'am."

"Perhaps gadfeathers might make good slipgizzles because of their wandering ways."

"Brilliant! The Snow Rose might help us find them!" Hoole exclaimed, and then continued quietly as if thinking aloud, "By Glaux — gadfeathers, polar bears, monks, who knows? Maybe even wolves! — we will bring the battle to them with alliances of our own, alliances beyond anything they ever dreamed of."

As soon as Strix Strumajen left, Hoole sent for Phineas and Theo. He was fluttering around in great agitation when the two young owls arrived. Hoole briefly explained his idea for a network of slipgizzles, some of whom might be gadfeathers and polar bears, spread throughout the owl kingdoms. He finished by telling them the sad story of Strix Strumajen's daughter, Emerilla, who had fought so bravely in the skirmish at the Ice Fangs. Hoole glanced at the ember. "It will take strategy, planning, and cunning to bring war to the enemy — not mere magic."

"But Hoole," Grank interrupted. "You should not go to the Northern Kingdoms. It is still too dangerous for you there. But you're certainly right about the Snow Rose. She might be useful."

Grank seemed unduly agitated to Hoole. He was perched near the ember and, instead of draining the Spotted Owl's energy as it had done long ago, it seemed to be infusing him with a nervous excitement.

"Nobody will want the Snow Rose to leave the tree," said Theo. "They love her voice too much."

"A small sacrifice for a great cause. This is what we are about here. Phineas, you could accompany her. You are not known in the Northern Kingdoms. And perhaps Theo could go to the Southern Kingdoms." Grank spoke rapidly.

"And I, as well — to the Southern Kingdoms," Hoole said firmly. He observed how Grank with this new nervous energy was taking over the planning and could not help but wonder if the ember was somehow influencing him. As he began to speak again, he watched the others to see if there were any noticeable differences in their behavior. "Also, I feel that it would be better if Phineas came with me to the Southern Kingdoms. He is, after all, from the Shadow Forest there. He knows the territory."

"Yes, you are right," Grank said immediately.

"And owls in the Northern Kingdoms really don't know me that well," Theo said. Theo's background was somewhat shrouded in mystery. He came from a remote firth, the Firth of Grundenspyrr off the Firth of Fangs, and only rarely mentioned his family.

Grank, appearing somewhat calmer, began to speak again. "If you are to be gone all that time, we will need to set up a system so I can get messages to you."

"How would that work?" Phineas said. "You won't know where we are."

"Dead drops," Grank answered.

Hoole and Joss blinked. Neither of them had even heard the words before.

"Dead drops?" Phineas asked in almost a whisper. "Aren't they dangerous? Haunted, some say."

"Nonsense! Just old owl tales. Dead drops" — Grank turned to Hoole and Joss to explain — "are seemingly healthy trees that fall in the prime of their life for no particular reason. Many owls are very suspicious of them — nachtmagen, they think. It is no such thing. I have made a study of dead drops, which I shall not bore you with now, but there are structural reasons for them to crash. In any case, they are the perfect spot for coded messages to be left. I will make up a map of the ones that I know throughout the various forests of the S'yrthghar. You must check them regularly. Cuthbert and Gemma on the watch branch are strong fliers. We can use them as messengers in addition to Joss."

"Excellent ideas, Grank. Thank you so much." Hoole was relieved that his old friend seemed to be himself once again. But when he regarded the others, they seemed to have a somewhat distant look in their eyes. Were they daunted by the task he had set for them? They appeared to be not quite focused. They needed to pay attention to what he was about to say. It was of vital importance.

Hoole inhaled sharply, then began to speak slowly and most gravely. "But there is one thing."

"What is that?" Grank asked.

"Time is not on our side. We must strike first, and by Short Light at the very latest. The Long Night will be our best ally." Long Night was the longest night of the year and it was preceded by the shortest day, Short Light. During the time surrounding these two days, the sun never rose more than a sliver above the horizon.

"But Short Light is hardly three moon cycles away," Joss said.

"I know," replied Hoole. "There is much to be done. And it will be done."

"By Short Light, then." Grank nodded.

"By Short Light," the other owls echoed.

They echo my thoughts but do they really agree? Hoole wondered. There was something mechanical in their response. Was this how subjects of an absolute ruler conducted themselves? He needed thinking owls, not owlipoppen, the little doll owls that parents gave their chicks to play with. Was the ember destroying their ability to think like individual owls, to question, to challenge? This was frightening. *Perhaps*, Hoole thought, *I should tuck the ember away*. He remembered the first night they had come to the island after the Battle in the Beyond and how the entire island and the tree seemed enveloped in a luminous light. He had wondered then if it was the moon or the ember that had cast that light and had questioned the limits, the reach of the ember's power. But there was no time for pondering right now — no time at all if they were to invade by Short Light.

So it was settled. They would depart on their missions the following evening. Grank would stay behind to act as Hoole's regent in his absence. He would inform the parliament of the plan and, while Hoole was gone, he would work on the secret chamber he was constructing with a Burrowing Owl in Grank's hollow. For it was there that Hoole had decided to hide the ember. Not in his own hollow, but in Grank's. *Whom can I trust if not Grank — Grank my mentor, Grank my foster father, Grank my guardian.*

CHAPTER EIGHT
A Mission for Half-hags

The katabats were just beginning to blow, and for Theo they were a robust, windy welcome to the kingdom that had once been his home. Some said that these tricky and tumultuous drafts from the north were the invisible wall that discouraged owls of the S'yrthghar Kingdoms from venturing to the N'yrthghar. Theo, however, found the winds bracing and enjoyed the sport they offered. Grank had provided him with the names of the polar bears to contact who might make good slipgizzles. Of special importance was one named Svenka who had been a close friend of the late Queen Siv. She was said at this time of year — autumn — to be making her way from her summer lodge on Dark Fowl Island to a remote firthkin not that far from Theo's former home in the Firth of Grundenspyrr. His gizzard pinched at the thought of his family. It had not been a happy hollow. His father was so strict. His mum a meek little thing and not that bright. Until his little brother, Shadyk, came along, Theo had borne the brunt of his father's rages. His father was a retired H'rathian Guardsman. Although he had never risen to the rank of officer himself, he dreamed that Theo would join the Guard and accomplish what he had not.

But Theo had had no taste for battle or a soldier's life. Quiet and studious, he had learned to read by visiting a Glauxian Brother. When his father discovered this, he was furious.

"They're cowards, moon calves, the lot of them! Lazy, good-for-nothing owls. Don't know an ice scimitar from a pile of yarped pellets."

"They're good owls. They just don't believe in violence," Theo had argued. "Their nature is that of restraint. Their passion is peace. Their heroism comes from their mercy. Their honor is found in resistance, their dignity in their humility."

"Oh, shut up, for Glaux's sake!" His father had raised a talon and swatted Theo across the hollow.

There had not been a word of protest from his mum, just a mournful sigh.

His older sister, Pye, had escaped the hollow as soon as she could and, much to her family's horror, they discovered that she had joined a troop of gadfeathers. Pye could take care of herself. It was his little brother, Shadyk, that Theo worried about. Undersized, rather clumsy, and with all the meekness of his mum, he had become the favorite target of his da's anger, who humiliated him in front of others, often beating him. Theo tried to protect the little fellow as best he could. But one night Theo and his da had a terrible row. Theo decided he could take it no longer and so he flew off.

When Theo had come to the island in the Bitter Sea and met Grank, he had found the father he had always yearned for. Then a few short weeks after his arrival, the egg Grank had kept so carefully sequestered in his hollow hatched and Hoole came into the world. Theo simply could not believe his luck. For him, it was as if he had found a new little brother, indeed almost a whole new family.

But for all this time, Theo had been haunted with guilt for abandoning his little brother to endure the cruelties of their father all by himself. Then he realized with a start that Shadyk would now be old enough to go off on his own. He must have done so by this time.

Theo was concentrating so hard that he did not pick up the haggish stench of crow that was but a whiff on the edges of the tearing winds.

But the hagsfiend of the Ice Narrows rarely missed a creature who passed her way. Kreeth backed quickly into her cave as she saw Theo rounding a bend in the channel.

"Lutta, get out there. Remember the camouflage lessons I've taught you?"

"Yes, Auntie." Kreeth had settled upon "Auntie" as the term of endearment Lutta should use when addressing her.

"Code S-S-S."

"Snowy-Slender-Still," Lutta confirmed.

"Get out there and do it. Keep one eye closed, the other a slit, and alert your half-hags. Then report back to me."

"Yes, Auntie."

"Be quick about it. He's almost here."

Lutta didn't pause to ask who Kreeth wanted her to watch. She immediately turned as white as a Snowy Owl, then stepped outside the cave and arranged herself on the ice shelf. Intentionally wilfing, she narrowed her body by pressing her feathers close to her sides and stood as tall as possible. She appeared to be just another icicle among the many that hung like a fringed ice curtain in front of the cave. Within seconds, she spied the Great Horned. *A strong flier,* she noticed. He seemed to be accustomed to the north winds. When he had disappeared around another bend, she lifted her wings slightly and dispatched her half-hags to track him. "No poison," she ordered. A small swarm of them flew forth.

Half-hags possessed the uncanniest abilities to interpret and detect the faintest changes or traces in an air current disturbed by the wings of a passing owl. A tiny filament of down still spinning in the eddies, the musty odor of a pellet yarped in flight, nothing was too minuscule, too insignificant for the half-hags to detect.

"So what did you find out?" Kreeth asked when Lutta returned.

"Excellent flier. Appears to be used to the katabats. Heading on a course that will take him over the Ice Dagger."

Kreeth nodded.

"Appears to have come from the south."

"That's obvious," Kreeth said scathingly.

"But wait! The half-hags report that they picked up traces of a very strange sort of tree, one they have never detected from any bird coming out of the S'yrthghar."

Kreeth's dark, crowish eyes became little pinpricks of blackness that had the intensity of the brightest light. Excitement stirred within Lutta at the sight of her mistress's eyes. She knew that Kreeth was impressed. Her half-hags had performed brilliantly. "Very interesting!" Kreeth said in a raw whisper. "You must continue to follow him — discreetly. Send out your half-hags. I want to know everything." She paused. "I repeat, *everything*."

"Yes, Auntie," Lutta replied.

"And, dearie?"

"Yes, Auntie?"

"Your mother was renowned for the excellence of her half-hags. I wager that yours will be twice as good."

There was a slight rustle deep within Lutta's feathers. It was the murmur of the half-hags stirring in poisonous pleasure.

CHAPTER NINE

Theo Meets Svenka

"She's dead? Siv is really dead?" The polar bear swung her massive head from side to side as if trying to make sense out of these words.

Theo nodded. "I am sorry to bring you this sad news." He had found the polar bear Svenka in an inlet off the Firth of Fangs. Just before Theo left, Hoole had visited his forge at the great tree and seen in the flames of the forge's fires what he felt was surely Svenka and her cubs swimming north by northwest.

"Mum, did Auntie Siv die?" Rolf asked. Svenka's cubs, Rolf and Anka, were now almost half as big as their mother. Siv nodded and both the cubs began crying.

"We'll never see her again," Anka gasped in disbelief.

Theo knew he must give the kind bear her time to grieve, but the urgency of his mission pressed upon him. His gizzard began to twitch nervously. He must set up the slipgizzling system. Every moment was precious. Information was desperately needed to plan the invasion.

"But you say that they finally did meet as mother and son?" Svenka asked.

"Yes. She died folded in his wings." Theo was beginning to feel desperate. He could sense the minutes slipping through his talons. But Svenka and her cubs were there before him, awash in grief. He turned to the twin cubs and, remembering what Grank had said to comfort Hoole at his mother's death, repeated it to Rolf and Anka. "Siv and her son will meet again in glaumora," he said, "— in owl heaven."

The cubs instantly looked toward their mother. "But . . ." Anka blinked with confusion. "If Siv is in owl heaven and we are in bear heaven, we won't see her there, either."

"Don't worry, child," Theo said. "There are no separate heavens. All creatures are together. We just call them by different names."

"But you have not come merely to tell me of the death of my dear friend," Svenka said.

A feeling of great relief swept through Theo. "No. I have been sent by Hoole. Are you familiar with the term 'slipgizzle'?"

"Spy," Svenka said with more than a hint of unpleasantness in her voice.

"Yes." Theo paused. "I'm not asking that you go out and

spy, but just to keep your ears open." *And,* Theo thought, *those are rather large ears.* "There is not much time, Svenka. The last of the H'rathian troops were forced out of the palace by Lord Arrin. And now rumors abound that hagsfiends have formed an entire division — of just hagsfiends."

"A division of hagsfiends!" There was a flash of alarm in Svenka's dark eyes.

Theo nodded. The notion of King H'rath's Ice Palace falling to hagsfiends was as unthinkable to a polar bear as it was to any decent owl in the N'yrthghar. "Winter is setting in. The more water that freezes, the safer the hagsfiends are and the more vulnerable we are. Hoole is planning an invasion, a massive one. It has to happen on or before the Long Night. And we need all the information we can get, as fast as we can get it."

Svenka shook her head heavily as if despairing. "But we bears are solitary creatures. We do not hear much news."

"Oh, Mum," Rolf said, almost dancing off the iceberg with excitement. "I heard that a school of blueskins had been swimming out of the firthkin." He turned to Theo.

"And I heard a seal talking about anchovies in the ice gut that connects this firthkin to the big firth," Anka said.

"Cubs! Cubs!" Svenka interrupted. "I don't think schooling fish is the information that our friend Theo has in mind."

"Well, that is all very interesting," Theo said politely, thinking that such information could be quite helpful in tracking other polar bears who might agree to become part of the slipgizzle network.

"What exactly do you want to find out?" Svenka said.

"There is an owl with King Hoole, a very brave owl and good fighter — Strix Strumajen of the Ice Regiment. Her daughter, although very young, decided to fight, as well, but was lost in a skirmish off the Ice Fangs. We want to know if she is still alive."

Svenka shuddered. She was all too familiar with hags-fiends' habits. Just before her cubs were born, she had witnessed the murder of Myrrthe, Siv's beloved servant. Never would she forget the image of that hagsfiend flying off with the huge white Snowy's head impaled on the ice pike, still bleeding, leaving a trail like that of a bloody comet.

"And," Theo interrupted her grim recollections, "we need to learn all we can about the movements of hags-fiends and Lord Arrin." Theo went on to tell Svenka about the great tree and how Hoole was starting a new order. "You see, Svenka," Theo continued, "King Hoole is a very different sort of king. He does not want to be an absolute ruler. Despite the fact that he now possesses the greatest of all powers — the ember — he does not want to rule by any kind of magic — nachtmagen or otherwise. Hoole says that the true roots of power must be the ideals of goodness, equality, and nobility."

Svenka pondered the ways of hagsfiends and this young king. "I will find out what I can," she told Theo.

A deep quietness descended upon them and if the wind had not picked up, they might have heard the soft whispers of the half-hags' wings.

"What!" Kreeth screeched. "He wants to rid the world of magic? What an idiot!" She began to croak madly with laughter, then she turned serious. "But that ember! That ember! I must have it. It is wasted on this stupid king. It will be wasted on any creature, save myself." Her eyes became dark pinpricks as the old hagsfiend began to dream of spells never imagined, of curses and enchantments never conceived. "Well, my dear, we have our work cut out for us. Now, tell me, have you practiced your Spotted Owl transformation lately?"

CHAPTER TEN

Into the S'yrthghar

"**B**ut I can't sing!" Hoole protested.

"Nor could your mother, my dear. Just hum along," the Snow Rose said as she tucked a few random feathers and some twigs into the fan of Hoole's tail. *My goodness*, she thought, *I am actually tucking a feather into the back plumage of a king! Imagine a gadfeather dressing a king! A little tizzy in the old gizzy*, she chuckled silently to herself.

The Snow Rose then turned to Phineas. "The same goes for you. I'll do the melody. You do the harmony. Let's hope no one asks us to sing. Remember, we're going to plead sore throats — or at least the two of you are."

It had been Grank's idea that Hoole, like his mother, should go disguised as a gadfeather on this flight into the Southern Kingdoms. Although few had seen Hoole, there was always the chance that some owl might recognize him. When three gadfeathers set off from the great tree, no owl would suspect a king was among them.

Soon Cape Glaux loomed ahead of the trio on the far side of the sea, which the owls of the tree had taken to calling the Sea of Hoolemere.

Their mission was twofold: to get news of Emerilla and to recruit slipgizzles. They lighted down on the tip of Cape Glaux. "Where to go?" Phineas sighed. "Where to begin?"

"A grog tree," the Snow Rose said quickly. "That's where one gets all the news or gossip. There are bound to be some gadfeathers there and perhaps a few old perch warriors."

"Perch warriors?" Hoole and Phineas asked together.

"Perch warriors. Never heard the expression?" The Snow Rose blinked. Phineas and Hoole both shook their heads. "Well, some are veterans, but many of them have never been to war. Of course, they won't admit that. Mostly they perch in grog trees quaffing great quantities of bingle juice and clacking their beaks about war, old battles, and notions about how they should have been fought. Moments of great valor, usually their own. They are either too old or too lazy for war now, but they have very definite ideas about it. Glaux forbid they should actually ever have to get off their perches and fly into battle. But they are all for sending the young'uns off."

"Hmmph!" Hoole gave a snort of disapproval.

"Yes, I know," the Snow Rose said. "But they are a very

good source of information. Some of it could be quite helpful. They'll talk to anyone. If there has been word of a Spotted Owl from the N'yrthghar who is missing in action, they will know about her. And if there has been a Glauxian Brother around, they will know about him, too." Here the Snow Rose gave Hoole a look, for he had spoken to her and Theo about his wish to enlist Brother Berwyck in their cause. "They have great contempt for the brothers."

"Because they don't fight?" Hoole affectionately thought of dear old Brother Berwyck, who had taught him how to fish when he was still quite young, Brother Berwyck who had come to the S'yrthghar some time ago on a pilgrimage.

"Exactly."

"Well, where's the nearest grog tree?" Phineas asked.

"I believe there is one on the border between Silverveil and the Shadow Forest. But it's getting on toward morning. What with crows and all, I think we should wait until tween time." Hoole and Phineas sighed impatiently. *These young owls,* the Snow Rose thought. "Now, don't fret. The days are growing shorter. Evening will be here before you know it. We have just enough time before twixt time to get something to eat."

It was good hunting on the cape. With few trees, prey

was easy to spot, and the rocky outcroppings and scrubby land was scampering with voles, mice, and the occasional rock rat, which were particularly succulent.

Phineas caught one that they shared but gave Phineas first choice since he was the one who had pounced on it.

"I say, Phineas," the Snow Rose nodded at the little Pygmy Owl. "You hunt right good for a little fella."

"Size has nothing to do with it," Hoole said. "It's all about accuracy. See where he punctured it — right between the eyes? Phineas has always been a great hunter. No one does the kill spiral like him."

A riffle of embarrassment stirred Phineas's feathers. The little Pygmy was a very modest owl and did not relish being the center of attention. "It was nothing," Phineas said as he tore off the head of the rock rat.

The spindly trees that grew on Cape Glaux offered no hollows, but beneath some of the large boulders that were scattered across the land, they found shelter from the wind and whatever random crows might be passing overhead.

So as night bleached into day, the three owls nestled beneath the overhang of a boulder and went to sleep. It was the first time that either Phineas or Hoole had ever slept on the ground. The Snow Rose, however, was used to such accommodations because Snowy Owls lived and nested in what they called ground scrapes. Just before falling asleep, the three owls were alone in their own thoughts.

The Snow Rose remembered a fox that she had once caught in Silverveil years before. It had been so long since she had tasted fox that her gizzard gave a little gurgle at the mere memory of it.

Phineas missed his own family's hollow and his parents and younger sister, who had all perished in a forest fire in the region known as Ambala.

Hoole reflected on how curious life could be. He had thought he was an orphan and then discovered that he had a mother. Then she died before he could even get to know her. He had thought he was an ordinary owl and now he was a king. Why had he been able to fetch that coal from the fiery mouth of the volcano? It had all happened in the midst of battle, the battle in which his mother had been dealt her mortal wound. Something had beckoned him during the battle. He had actually flown through a curtain of flames, which had not even singed him. But he did remember something now: The sides of the volcano had begun to turn transparent and that was how he saw the ember. This ember — was it a blessing or a curse? He knew deep in his gizzard that it could be very dangerous. He had seen the subtle changes that occurred in some owls when they were in its presence. He remembered all too well how Grank had become oddly agitated, and how Theo, Joss, and Phineas had replied to him in that queerly mindless way before they had left on their missions. As long as the ember was in his possession, however, he felt he could master whatever peculiar emanations it had and, for the most part, protect those around the ember from its influence. But what would happen after he was gone? Death did not frighten him anymore. He knew that his mother, Siv, would be waiting for him in glaumora. Death did not frighten him, but leaving the ember behind did.

His eyes grew heavy now. He must stop thinking about such things. How wonderful it would be if he could meet once more with Berwyck; how lovely, those lazy evenings of fishing back in Bitter Sea on the island, the two of them perched on the limb of an alder that hung out over the pond. The moonlight scattered across the surface of the dark water, and the fish stirring beneath — just waiting to be caught. There was no ember then. He did not know even what a mother really was exactly, and he certainly had no notion of kingship. Life was very, very simple then. Hoole yawned and fell fast asleep as if into a dense fog.

The fog thinned to a mist, and from the mist flew a lovely Spotted Owl. Her spots seemed to shimmer. She looked battle weary but strong. Hoole's gizzard sang. *What a warrior!* And she was flying straight into another skirmish. *I must help her*, he thought. He spread his wings and took off. It was hard to see her. Was the fog thickening now? Was it not fog but the Short Light? Was the Short Light here already? Impossible. Not yet. Hagsfiends? Were they doing this? Was their magic so powerful that they could change the moon cycles? Every time he sensed the Spotted Owl close by, the fog would thicken more. He lost sight of her. The spots of her plumage, which moments ago twinkled with the brightness of the stars, faded away. Now the fog turned dark. Not dark like the night, but a crowish darkness, and didn't he smell a terrible stench? And almost as soon as he thought this, a dreadful yellow light seeped out of the dark. *Great Glaux, it's the fyngrot — I am going yeep!*

Then the shadow of an owl with a misshapen wing blocked the awful yellow light. It was his mum!

"Mum, where are you?"

"Hold steady, my prince. Hold steady."

"I can't! I can't!"

"Hoole, wake up! Wake up!" The Snow Rose was shaking him hard, so hard that a small storm of her feathers swirled across his blinking eyes. *Just like the fog*, he thought.

Phineas was standing next to her, looking quite frightened. "You were having a bad dream, I think. Sorry about the feathers," the Snow Rose apologized, "but I'm just getting ready for a mid-season molt."

Phineas hopped over. "Are you all right? What was it?"

"A bad dream, I guess," Hoole replied.

"What was it about?" Phineas pressed.

"I can't really remember. Something about fog, I think, because when I saw Rose's feathers, I thought I was still flying in the fog." He paused and raised a talon to scratch his head, then gave himself a little poke in his belly feathers near his gizzard in an attempt to jolt his memory. "For the life of me, I can't remember what the dream was about. But it wasn't all bad," he said. It was as though a wisp of something sweet and dear had blown through that dream. "Is it tween time yet?" he asked.

"Just," the Snow Rose replied. The three owls peeked out from under the overhang. The sky to the west was purpling and streaked with clouds of burning orange. The moon was just rising behind the clouds, which cast an eerie yellow light on it. Hoole felt a twinge in his gizzard and a riffle passed through his feathers. Phineas looked up at his friend. "Scroom fly over your deathspot?"

"Huh?" asked Hoole.

"For Glaux's sake, he's spooked enough!" the Snow Rose scolded.

"It's just an old saying from Ambala. It doesn't mean anything," Phineas said apologetically.

"I only wish it were a scroom," Hoole replied cryptically.

"Now, what do you mean by that?" Phineas asked.

Hoole gave a soft churring sound. "You know, I'm not quite sure. But let's get on with our business."

So, as the orange clouds were engulfed in purple, and the purple darkened to black, the owls rose into the night along with the first stars.

CHAPTER ELEVEN

Perch Warriors

"So, as I was saying, I had just confronted that young lieutenant who didn't know his pin feathers from his flight feathers, 'That ain't the way you fight these creatures — begging your pardon, sir,' I told him. 'When you got them hagsfiends with their cursed fyngrots, you chase them toward open water.' So that's exactly what we did. I took charge of the operation and . . .'"

Hoole, the Snow Rose, and Phineas had alighted in the grog tree, just as the Great Horned Owl had begun to hold forth. When he finished, he turned to the three new arrivals. "Bless my gizzard, what have we here? Three gadfeathers. Come from the north, did you?"

"Any good fighting up there?" a Great Gray asked. Hoole recognized him. He had come with the hireclaws Siv had gathered when she had flown to the Beyond for that last battle. He hoped that the Great Gray would not recognize him in his gadfeather disguise.

"Good fighting in the north," a Barred Owl interrupted.

"I'll say. Me cousin says that the Glacier Palace has been invaded by hagsfiends led by a young hothead. Some claim he's mad." Hoole felt his gizzard still.

The Great Gray turned to the Snow Rose and Phineas, ignoring Hoole, for which he was thankful. "Then you fellas missed the big battle down here. In the Beyond," the Great Gray said. "Spectacular. I'll never forget the sight of the young king coming through that wall of flames with the ember." Hoole wilfed a bit and kept his head low between his shoulders. "Some bingle juice, will you? And some for my friends here." The Great Gray summoned the grog tree keeper, a disreputable-looking Screech Owl, who arrived with nutshells that held the potent liquid. They would only pretend to drink the juice. Hoole, Phineas, and the Snow Rose had to keep their heads clear.

Just then, a completely Trufynkken Short-eared Owl staggered through the air. "Another one, please, Harry! Medicinal purposes, you know."

"She was wounded up on the H'rathghar. Lost half of one foot," a Barred Owl whispered to Hoole and Phineas. They looked at her port-side foot, which had only two talons left.

"Must make hunting hard," Hoole said.

"We look after her. She should lay off the juice a bit, though," the Barred Owl said.

"Whatcha be sayin' about me, Alastair?" The Short-eared Owl suddenly spun her head around. Some bingle juice spat out with her words.

"Nothing, dear. Nothing."

"It is for medicinal purposes — the brother who tended me when I got down here said ... He said to me ... 'Lolly, darlin', nothing like a little touch of the old bingle to ease the pain, especially when winter comes on.'"

"Brother! A Glauxian Brother?" Hoole asked.

"Well, certainly not my own. Me own brother ain't worth a seagull's splat." Hearty laughter roared through the tree and shook the branches. A couple of the smaller owls, who could not hold their bingle juice, fell from the tree and, though half Trufynkken, managed to recover flight before slamming into the ground.

"Do you recall his name?" Hoole asked.

"Uh ... uh ..." She shook her head in short little jogs as if trying to rearrange her brain. "Wyckber, I think. Either Wyckber or Berwyck."

"Berwyck!" Hoole said. "A Boreal, right?"

"Yes, yes. That he be. A Boreal."

"Where can we find him?"

"Oh, dear, now — that could be a problem." Again she jogged her head around. "Let's see. I was pretty tired when I finally made it out of the N'yrthghar, but luckily had tailwinds. But I imagine . . . oh, yes, I probably made it well into Silverveil. 'Cause I wouldn't want to stop on the cape for long. No real trees, you know. Oh, it's coming back to me!" Lolly's amber eyes brightened, and she looked slightly less tipsy. "It was near that place where the Others done lived before they vanished. One of them whatchama-callits."

"Church?" Alastair the Barred Owl prompted.

"Yes, that be it."

"Lovely old place."

"There be ruins from the Others all through Silverveil," the Great Gray spoke up.

When Hoole had first come to the S'yrthghar, there had been no time to linger. They had had to fly straight to the Beyond, but he had always longed to see these strange hollows of the Others.

"Well, we'd best be on our way if we hope to find him," the Snow Rose said.

"Not before a song you don't." The Great Horned, the perch warrior who had been expounding on his war-time experiences in the N'yrthghar, spoke up. "You know, before we went into battle, old King H'rath always had some gadfeathers in to give us a rousing tune."

"What a bunch of rubbish," the Snow Rose muttered.

"What are we going to do?" Phineas whispered desperately.

"Leave it to me." The Snow Rose stepped out on the branch where she perched. "My two friends here are not in voice right now, having just come through their mid-season molt with slight sore throats." There was a murmur of understanding that swirled through the tree. It was, of course, a bit of nonsense, but these tipsy owls were ready to believe almost anything. "And I myself know few battle tunes. But I might sing you a song of ice and sky." This met with great approval, and the night swelled with hurrahs and cheers.

The Snow Rose began to sing. Her lovely voice flowed into the night of liquid moonlight and wove through the grog tree, making everything seem to shimmer.

> *Where the ice meets the sky,*
> *where the trees never grow,*
> *where the water is locked,*
> *so still, forever slow.*
> *Where the wind scours the land,*
> *carving bridges, spires, and peaks,*
> *listen closely, my friend,*
> *and you'll hear the ice speak.*

It speaks of times gone by,
creatures frozen in the deep.
Of a place where time grows still,
a place of long eternal sleep,
where the ice never melts
and the trees never grow.
That is where I long to fly —
I have ice crystals in my soul.

The last notes had hardly floated into the air before the three owls had taken wing.

"Phew! That was a close one!" Phineas sighed as he felt the sweet billow of a warm thermal curl under his wings.

CHAPTER TWELVE

Theo Pushes On

The polar bear sat on her haunches and regarded the Great Horned Owl. He was an honest fellow if there ever was one and, though this spying business did not appeal to her, she knew it was for a good cause. Her loyalty to the memory of Siv required that she do everything in her power to support Siv's son, the young king who seemed so good. "Theo," she began, "I will keep an eye out for you here. But the bear you really need to meet is Svarr, the father of my cubs. He lives up near Lord Arrin's stronghold in the eastern side of the Firth of Fangs. He knows a lot. He might know where to find this spotted owl, Emerilla, whom you seek."

"Where is this stronghold of Lord Arrin?"

"When you leave this inlet, head north and continue flying up the Firth of Fangs. It will grow narrow, then widen again, and just before it reaches a large lagoon, it narrows a second time. At this second set of narrows, fly east, following a tickle."

"A tickle?"

"Well, a firthkin is a small firth, and a tickle is even smaller than a firthkin. Polar bears call it that because when we swim such narrow passageways, it is barely wide enough for us to pass through and it tickles our sides sometimes."

Theo blinked. He had never thought of these enormous creatures with their thick fur and tough hides as being ticklish.

"Then at the end of the firthkin where the ice piles up, there is a cave. That is where you can find Svarr."

"And you say it is close to where Lord Arrin has his stronghold?"

"Yes. But it's not the closeness. It's the smee holes that are important."

"Smee holes? Why are they important?"

"We polar bears love smee holes. We love the hot steam that comes from them and the lovely thermal baths that surround them. Svarr especially loves them. He's getting on a bit and has a touch of stiffness in his shoulders. The hot water helps. Anyhow, a long time ago, polar bears discovered that smee holes conduct sound very easily. Svarr is a nosy sort of fellow and he found it interesting to listen in on various conversations, if indeed any were going on while he was soaking. I went to visit him myself several moon cycles back on behalf of Siv to learn what Lord

Arrin was up to. Svarr will be able to help you." She paused. "And, by the way, give him my best and tell him that in two years we can meet up again. Same time, same place."

Theo thanked Svenka and spread his wings. Just as he was about to loft himself into the air, he heard the cubs. "Mum, can we swim with him just to the end of the firthkin?"

"Oh, all right, but don't you dare go out into the big firth. Promise?"

"We promise!" they chorused.

Theo flew low and the cubs, swimming on their backs below, babbled on the entire time.

"Don't you think it's unfair that Mum won't let us see any battles?"

"Yeah, she never lets us do anything except sit at seal holes and bash them when they come up."

"It was fun at first, but then it got boring."

"Have you ever fought in a battle, Theo?"

"Well, yes, and I didn't much like it."

"How come?" Rolf asked. "Were you scared?"

"Of course I was scared. You'd have to be yoicks not to be."

"Yoicks?" Rolf asked.

"You remember, Rolf, Auntie Siv used to say that all the time. It's like polar bears say 'blairn,' and owls say 'yoicks.'"

"And now," said Theo, "for this owl it is time to say good-bye. Be good cubs and turn around and swim back."

"All right." They both sighed. "Bye, Theo."

"Bye, Rolf. Bye, Anka."

It was close to midnight by the time Theo reached the end of the tickle, and it *was* narrow. But just before the end, he spotted the most immense bear he had ever seen. Could this be Svarr? The bear was sitting upright and looking down at something. Theo flew lower. The bear heard him, raised a paw, made a soft patting motion on the air, and then drew the paw to his muzzle as if to indicate quiet. A dark head emerged from the hole and then there was a sudden *thwack* that reverberated into the night and caused the waters of the tickle to slosh violently. Blood spread across the ice before the bear had even hauled the seal from its hole.

"Be with you in a minute," he said as he proceeded to rake his middle claw down the seal's belly and neatly peel back the skin. He began scooping out the blubber.

"Mmmm-mmm, that is one tasty seal." He turned to look at Theo. "What can I do for you?"

"Are you Svarr?"

"Oh, no! What's she up to now?"

"Who?"

"Svenka."

"How'd you know?"

"Svenka has become quite social of late. Most un-bearish. She seems to consort with owls."

"Well, from what I understand, you know quite a bit about owls yourself," Theo said.

"Indeed, I do. But they don't know about me." The great bear looked amused.

"What interests you so about owls?" Theo was genuinely curious.

"Their politics, their wars, their scheming blairney ways. Very entertaining."

"Well, I count myself lucky for meeting you," Theo said amicably.

Svarr looked up for the first time at Theo. "I'm glad you didn't take offense."

"No offense. It's true. I really don't care for the politics myself. Or the war."

"So, why are you here, and where do you come from?"

"Originally, I come from the Firth of Grundenspyrr, not far from here."

"Good sealing up there."

"Yes. But now I come from another place in the S'yrthghar — the Southern Kingdoms. I come as an emissary of King Hoole."

Svarr put down a bloody hunk of blubber and opened his eyes wide. "You do, do you?"

Theo nodded.

"I hear the young king is a good sort. Fought bravely at the battle in Beyond the Beyond. And got some sort of magic ember. Maybe he could knock out the hagsfiends with it. Now that would be a blessing of Ursa!"

"You hear a lot, Svarr, and that is why I have come."

"Why's that?" Svarr was suddenly alert.

"What you hear could help our young king." Theo went on to explain Hoole's plan to have a network of slip-gizzles that could keep him informed.

"Well, you know polar bears, we've never taken sides. But these owls and their hagsfiends are a bad lot. I heard Svenka herself got caught in a fyngrot back before her cubs were born."

"Oh, that reminds me. I have a message from Svenka. She said in two years she would meet you. Same time, same place."

Svarr rolled his huge dark eyes. "What's a fella to do?" He sighed, and when he exhaled, it nearly blew Theo off the ice outcropping on which he perched. "So you want me to keep an ear open by the old smee holes?"

"Yes. Find out if Lord Arrin is planning a counterattack

of some sort. How many troops does he have? Any new hagsfiends?"

"Whooo-hee!"

Again Theo had to grip with his talons on the ice. He wished that Svarr did not indulge in such windy exclamations. "You, my fine friend, are behind the times. These days, Lord Arrin hardly has two yarped pellets to rub together."

"What?"

"You heard me."

"That last battle shattered his forces. They split like ice fields on a summer's day."

"You mean they're gone?"

"Not gone. Regrouped. They're all fighting for the spoils. It's a feast for vultures up here in the N'yrthghar. Before the Battle in the Beyond, Lord Arrin had taken old King H'rath's Ice Cliff Palace on the H'rathghar glacier, but now some upstart, with a force double the size of Arrin's, laid siege to it and drove Lord Arrin's forces out. Then Ullryck, a horrible hagsfiend if there ever was one — and Lord Arrin's best assassin — well, she up and starts a division of all her own hagsfiends. No owls at all."

"New alliances, eh?"

"Yes, new alliances. They are all struggling for power.

There is even a gang of old gadfeathers who have decided to fight."

"Gadfeathers fighting?" Theo was aghast.

"Shocking, isn't it? They don't call themselves gadfeathers anymore. They call themselves kraals. They're not so much interested in power or killing. They just like to steal, mostly."

"Kraals." Theo repeated the word. It must have come from the old Krakish word "kraalynk," which meant to attack for treasure.

"They've traded in their gaudy bits and bobs for paint and live in ground nests out on the tundra. They figured out how to make colored paints from berries, mosses, and the like. You've never seen anything like them. All painted up. Makes a gadfeather look plain, I tell you!"

"And you say that some other group has taken over the palace on the H'rathghar glacier?" Theo asked.

"Yes. Can't remember the fellow's name. And he has hagsfiends with him. Young ones, from what I hear."

Svarr had definitely heard a lot, Theo reflected. But the most important piece of information was that the N'yrthghar was in shambles. A feast for vultures, indeed, with outlaws and kraals and hagsfiends and tyrants all competing for the spoils. He needed to visit the Ice Cliff

Palace now to find out just how many owls and hagsfiends were holding it.

"Oh, I nearly forgot," Theo said shortly before he left. "Have you heard of a Spotted Owl named Emerilla?"

"Emerilla, daughter of Strumajen and Hurthwel?"

"Yes! Yes!"

"Oh, indeed I have. She was said to be one of the finest young soldiers in the Ice Regiment, but it is thought she was lost in a battle. Never heard from again."

"You know nothing further of her?"

"No. But they talk about her all the time. Lord Arrin is obsessed with her. I think he'd like her for his mate. Some say she's gone off with the hagsfiends. Others claim she's with the kraals."

"Well, thank you, Svarr. You have been most helpful. And if you hear anything, might there be a way you could get news to us?"

"Well, as you know, we are a solitary sort. But I suppose I could get word to Svenka."

"That would be fine, because we will be checking in regularly with her."

"She's a good lass. I miss her sometimes. Tell her I'll look forward to our meeting in two years. Wish her well with the cubs."

"Would you like to send a special message to Rolf and Anka?"

"Rolf and Anka? Now why in the name of Ursa did she name them that? Those are the two most un-bearish names I've ever heard. We are always called good north-country names like Sven or Svarr."

"Maybe she just wanted to try something different, original," Theo suggested.

Svarr crinkled one eye shut and pawed at his chin fur. "You know, sometimes I think these females try to be just a little too original, don't you?"

"Oh, I wouldn't know, really. But is there anything you want to tell the cubs?"

"No, not really. Cubs rather bore me."

Theo blinked. No doubt, polar bears were an odd species. He thanked Svarr again and took off. *Now*, he wondered, *should I fly on and see them, Mum? Da? Shadyk?*

The mere thought of his father made him flinch and his wings feel heavy as stone.

CHAPTER THIRTEEN

Home?

The Firth of Grundenspyrr was as crooked as a wolf's hind leg, and it was one of the few firths that had trees. Just as the dawn was breaking, Theo spotted the N'yrthfyr birch that had been the tree where his family had its hollow. Theo was unsure exactly how to announce his arrival. His mother was a frail sort and he didn't want to shock her. He wondered if Shadyk was still there. He thought it might be best to fly around to the back of the tree where there was a tiny hollow that had not been used in years. If it was empty, he would just slip in and listen to what was going on with his own family for a while.

He could hear voices as he approached the back of the tree: one male and one female. He squashed into the hollow, which was more suitable for an Elf or Pygmy owl than himself. His mother had always had a tiny, meek voice, but now there was an earsplitting din coming from his family's hollow. And shrill peals of laughter.

"By my butt feathers, that's the funniest thing I ever heard," the female said.

"But Philma, it's true!"

Philma! That was Theo's mum's name, but he had never heard her laugh, let alone speak so coarsely. And the other voice was definitely not his father's, nor was it Shadyk's. *What in Glaux's name is going on here?* Theo wasted no time in wondering. He immediately flew out of the tiny hollow and around the tree, lighting down on a branch. "Mum!" The word was swallowed in gales of raucous laughter. "Mum! Mum!" he shouted out. The laughter stopped. Two bright, sparkling yellow eyes peeped from the hollow. Atop her head were the fluffy ear tufts that his mum was so proud of because they were fuller and lovelier than those of most Great Horned Owls. It was indeed his mum!

"Theo!" she hooted. "Theo, lovey! I can't believe it! Theo's come home! Wyg, get out here. It's Theo!"

Wyg? Who's Wyg? Theo racked his brain. Theo's father's name was Hakon. Another Great Horned stepped out onto the branch. "Mum, where's Da?"

"Oh, dear. How to break this to you."

"Now, now, Philma." Wyg was preening her ear tufts with what seemed to Theo an overly familiar gesture.

"Your da, I regret to say" — although there did not

seem to be much regret in her voice — "has done passed on, Theo."

"You mean died? He's dead?"

"Yes, dearie. I know how much he meant to you."

She's got to be kidding! thought Theo.

"What happened?"

"Well, when Shadyk went off to fight in the wars . . ."

"What? Shadyk went off to fight?"

"Yes. Can you believe it? He's made quite a name for himself. But I'll tell you about that later. Come on in the hollow. We just got some fresh-killed lemmings." She turned and blinked rapidly at Wyg. "Wyg is such a hunter." She flew up and tweaked one of his ear tufts. Then they nuzzled a bit. At this point, Theo could have been knocked over by a feather.

"You were saying about Da?" Theo asked.

"Oh, yes, dear. I do get distracted." She giggled.

Has there ever been a jollier widow? Theo wondered.

"Well, when Shadyk went off to the glacier battles, your father, you know, never one to be outdone — especially by a son whom he'd always considered the runt — well, he decided to go, too." She paused and tried to rearrange her merry face into a somewhat more doleful expression.

"Yes," Theo said, "and what happened?"

"So he went off and got himself killed — right off the

twig, practically. Hardly had a chance to raise his ice blade." She cast her eyes down mournfully, made a sound halfway between a whimper and a sigh. Then she looked up, her eyes beaming as Theo had never seen them. "But now I have a new mate. And he don't swat me — no, not never — like your da sometimes did."

Theo was astonished beyond anything. "Well, I'm so happy for you. And what's this about Shadyk? You said he's gone off to the wars?"

Now Philma's eyes grew large. "Oh, my goodness, he certainly did. And he's not so little anymore." Her voice dropped. "Theo, dear, you're not going to believe this, but Shadyk started himself up a regiment. And guess what?"

"What?" Theo was afraid to ask.

"They have captured H'rath's old Ice Palace."

This was truly beyond belief. Theo blinked his eyes several times. "The Ice Palace of the H'rathghar glacier?"

"The very one." Philma nodded.

"But Mum, that was King H'rath's. He was a good king."

"Well, you know how these things go, dear," his mum replied.

"No, Mum. I don't know."

"Well, King H'rath was defeated, and that awful Lord Arrin came and took it over. But he doesn't know how to run anything, Shadyk says, and it's a shame to let that beautiful palace go to waste."

"To waste? Mum, Shadyk has to be a king to live there. What in the world does Shadyk know about running anything?"

"He'll learn, dear. He'll learn. And you know he has the nicest group of young hagsfiends."

"Hagsfiends! He has hagsfiends?"

"Why, yes, dear. You know, they're not as bad as you might think, especially the young ones. He's training them, bringing them up right and proper."

Proper hagsfiends? Madness! There were tens, hundreds of questions Theo was dying to ask. Had Shadyk or his mum no loyalty to Siv or H'rath? To Hoole? They had certainly heard about Hoole and the Battle in the Beyond. Had Shadyk no reservations about hagsfiends? But as soon as Theo found out about his brother's alliance with the creatures he knew that these questions could not be asked. And even more important, he knew that he must not under any circumstances reveal that he was an ally and close friend to King Hoole, the rightful heir to the throne of the N'yrthghar.

"We go up there all the time to the Glacier Palace," his mother continued. "They treat us like royalty."

It was all Theo could do to keep from yarping. But

suddenly, he realized this was his chance. He composed himself as best he could. "I would love to see Shadyk again."

"Well, we could all go for a visit. What fun!" Philma lofted herself straight up into the air and beat her talons together in a gesture of utter joy. Theo was stunned. *Imagine celebrating a son who was consorting with hagsfiends.*

CHAPTER FOURTEEN

A Stench Most Foul

"Keep a sharp lookout for smoke," Hoole said as he, Phineas, and the Snow Rose flew in a southeasterly direction over the Forest of Ambala. The three owls had been in the Southern Kingdoms almost two moon cycles now. At the moment, they were looking for the telltale signs of a blacksmith's forge, or Rogue smith, as these independent ironmongers had already come to be called.

The news had quickly spread throughout the S'yrthghar of the powerful new weapons that Hoole and Theo and a few others had fought with in the Battle of the Beyond. In the few moon cycles since then, Hoole was amazed to see several of the hireclaws who had fought for Siv trying their luck diving for coals and building fires. A few of them had actually become proficient at it. But then they were faced with the harder task of trying to figure out what seemed like magic to them — melting rock into metal and making weapons from it. But most important, the new Rogue smiths and colliers were all passionately devoted to the late Queen Siv. Loners by nature, they avoided settling down. That did not mean they were completely unsociable. They genuinely liked it when visitors stopped by their forges and admired their fires or their ironwork. And they became positively chatty when discussing blacksmithing.

Hoole quickly ascertained that Rogue smiths would make excellent slipgizzles. Every owl now craved battle claws and came to them in hopes of procuring a set, so the smiths heard plenty of news. A forge could yield as much information as a grog trée these days. Hoole decided early on that they would not directly ask the owls if they wanted to be slipgizzles. He would first determine a smith's loyalties and secondly assess if he or she had the wits and instincts for collecting information and passing it along. Invariably, they did have these qualities and were thrilled to be of service to the noble young king. Hoole recognized many of them from the battle, but luckily they did not recognize him in his gadfeather disguise.

As he, the Snow Rose, and Phineas flew into the night, Hoole reflected on what he had learned so far. There definitely were hagsfiends around. But no one knew quite where. There were stories of a black feather here and there, or a rank crowish scent carried on a breeze. There were sightings of the queer black pellets they yarped.

But it was not only the information that Hoole and his friends picked up that was important. While they had been traveling, Hoole had the sudden inspiration that some of the more promising smiths should be encouraged to fly to the great tree to train under the watchful eye of Grank and Theo, when Theo returned to the tree. He let this information be revealed in a casual chatty way. "I hear," he said to one Rogue smith in Tyto, "that at the great tree, the one they call the Great Ga'Hoole Tree, which was named for the king, that one can learn colliering and smithing from the masters themselves." In this way Hoole managed to send a half dozen promising Rogue smiths and colliers to the tree to begin their training. There would be battle claws aplenty when the time was ripe!

On the border of Silverveil and The Barrens, Hoole, Phineas, and the Snow Rose had a rendezvous with Joss. Joss reported that Grank was delighted with the influx of smiths and colliers. There were now four forges going, with two smiths to a forge, so the supply of battle claws had quadrupled. New recruits for the invasion were arriving every day, and Lord Rathnik and his lieutenants were training them in the use of ice weapons. The ice weapons themselves were surviving well due to the cool weather and the preservative powers of the milkberry vines.

Hoole and Phineas, who for so long had watched Theo at his forge, learned to discreetly throw out suggestions and pointers while still being careful to conceal their true identities. It was in this way that Hoole, Phineas, and the Snow Rose forged their own strong bonds with these owls. Most important, they wanted to know if any hagsfiends had been spotted in the Southern Kingdoms who were known to be aloof, reluctant even to reveal their name. Repeatedly the answer was no. Not one had been spotted. But in his gizzard, Hoole had twinges of doubt.

"But we would have smelled something if they had been around," Phineas said.

"Oh, that crowish odor!" exclaimed the Snow Rose. She would never forget the terrible stench of hagsfiends in the Battle of the Beyond. "You never get used to it."

"But owls don't have the best sense of smell," Hoole argued.

And then one night when they were visiting a Rogue smith in Ambala, Hoole saw something in the fire there that made his gizzard lurch. It was a hagsfiend! Hoole knew it as certainly as he had known anything.

Phineas immediately realized that Hoole had spotted danger in the fire. The Rogue smith was looking at Hoole peculiarly. "What's wrong with your friend?" In that same moment, the first wave of the crowish stench filled the darkening night, and then the blackness of that night began to fade into yellow, and the yellow grew stronger as the outer edge of a fyngrot rolled in like a rising tide.

"We have no weapons!" Phineas whispered. They must do something before the hagsfiend launched its half-hags with their poisonous loads. To do that, however, the hagsfiend had to be in range. It was the fyngrot, which was cast like a deadly net, that brought a victim into range and stilled the victim so the half-hags could take aim.

"No ice sabers," said the Rogue smith.

Hoole seized a poker from the forge. It had the sphere of molten iron at its tip. Time seemed to slow and events happened in a dreamlike, liquidy way. But Hoole's thoughts came clearly and distinctly. With his mother, he had escaped a fyngrot in the Battle of the Beyond. "Hold steady, my prince. Hold steady," Siv had said then. In an unparalleled act of willpower she rendered them both impenetrable to the effects of the fyngrot.

And now it was Hoole's turn. He did not have his father's ice scimitar, but he had the image of his mother, and in his talon the poker with the molten iron at its tip. He raised the poker and charged through the yellow light, slashing at the hagsfiend. The stink of singed feathers now mixed with the crowlike smell. Then the hagsfiend suddenly looked quite ordinary. The fyngrot faded, and there was a soft plop. No more yellow — just a pile of black feathers on the ground in front of the forge.

"Look!" Phineas said in a stunned voice. "It's just like an ordinary crow."

"It's so small," whispered the Snow Rose.

"I'd never believe it," said the Rogue smith. "It ain't even half the size it was." Hagsfiends' wingspans were enormous, three times that of the largest owls, and now this bird seemed the same size — if that — of a crow.

"So finally we find one, after all the rumors," Hoole said. "Must have come by a land route. Not enough ice this time of year to risk a sea crossing." And once more Hoole thought how they must be ready to invade by Short Light.

Hoole stepped toward the body and prodded it with the poker so that it turned over. The four owls gasped. There was a shallow disc-shaped depression where its face should have been. But there were no eyes, no beak, and in the depression was a thin yellow liquid that was quickly evaporating to dust. It was shocking and horrible.

"However did you bring this creature down, Hoole?" Phineas asked.

"Hoole!" The Rogue smith gasped. "You are King Hoole?" The other three owls looked at one another as the Rogue smith fell to his knees. "I should have known."

"Rise up, smith," Hoole said. "Yes, I am the king."

"You saved us with your magic. A magic greater than the hagsfiend's. But you do not have the ember with you. The one they call the Ember of Hoole."

"It was not magic," Hoole said sharply. "It was the power of my will, my gizzard. I used no magic at all. Good smith, you are right. I do not have the ember with me. I had a poker forged in your own fires, with a hunk of molten white-hot metal at its tip. But smith, promise me this: Tell no one that I am the king."

"Your Majesty, I give you my word of honor." He paused. His pale yellow eyes locked with Hoole's deep amber ones. "I give you my name and such is my honor: Rupert is my name."

Hoole knew after his time in the Southern Kingdoms and having met a score of Rogue smiths that the knowledge of a smith's name was a trust not lightly given.

So the young king bowed his head to Rupert and said simply, "I am honored, Rupert."

CHAPTER FIFTEEN

Black Feathers in the Desert

Phineas thought he smelled the telltale stench. He had been skimming close to the low-growing bushes and scanning the nettles and spiny shrubs that grew in this region bordering the Desert of Kuneer when he had sighted a small ball of dark fluff and then caught the unmistakable whiff. He lighted down next to the shrub.

"Look," said Phineas.

"What?" asked Hoole, lighting down next to him.

"Small feathers, black ones, pin feathers," Phineas replied.

"What is it?" asked the Snow Rose.

"Tumbledown," Phineas said. Tumbledown was the delicate fluffy underfeathers of a bird. So light were these feathers that when molted, they would blow away and get caught up in tall grass or shrubs. With most birds, the tumbledown was pale in color, but this was black. Phineas looked up at his mates. "Tumbledown from a hagsfiend."

The three owls wilfed a bit. It was a long time before

anyone spoke. Hoole twisted his head nearly completely around and then settled his gaze to the southwest. "The Desert of Kuneer is very close, I think."

"A quarter night's flight at the most," the Snow Rose replied.

"It would make a perfect place for hagsfiends, wouldn't it?" Hoole asked. "Dry, landlocked, far from any sea." Water, especially salt water, was the only thing hagsfiends really feared. The N'yrthghar was the safe haven for hagsfiends because for most of the year the Everwinter Sea was frozen. So it made sense that if they came to the Southern Kingdoms that the Desert of Kuneer would offer refuge. But then again, the Beyond would also be safe. Far from any seas, it was a desert of sorts, too. Hoole wondered if any had gone there. They had certainly fought there. Yes, they had had to retreat, but could the wolves have kept them away?

Hoole shut his eyes for a long time and thought. Hagsfiends in the south. Rumors of the Ice Palace falling to new rebels. It would be a fight on all fronts. Hoole knew that unless forced to, they could not fight anywhere until they were ready. But they were less than two moon cycles away from Short Light. Still, it would be reckless to go into the Desert of Kuneer and hunt down hagsfiends now. Before passing out of Ambala into the desert, they had checked a dead drop. There had been a coded message from Grank asking about his progress and reporting that the rumor of an all-hagsfiend division led by Ullryk was true, though there had been no confirmation from either Joss or Theo that this division was the one holding the Ice Palace. All of this ran through Hoole's mind now. His gizzard was in a fever, but Short Light or no, he would not act rashly. He still needed more information.

"We need to turn back. I need to see Rupert again and have him build me a fire. I need some good flames to read."

And so they returned that very evening to Ambala.

"Back so soon?" Rupert looked up from his forge. "Don't tell me, more hagsfiends?"

Hoole nodded. "We think so. Rupert, I have a favor to ask."

"Anything at all," Rupert replied.

"I need your fire, Rupert."

Rupert looked perplexed. "Wanna try your hand at a bit of smithing, do you? Bet you're a natural."

"Well, no actually, Rupert — I have a certain gift for reading the flames." He looked now very seriously at Rupert. "It is a talent, Rupert. It is not magic. It is the same as when some owls are born with more sensitive gizzards and seem to sense things before they happen. That is the way it is with me and flames. Might I use your fire?"

Rupert stepped away. "It is all yours, Hoole."

"And one more thing, might you give that rock on top of the vent a shove? I would like the fire to get some more air and build up the flames a bit."

Within a very few minutes, great towering flames were leaping from the crack in the boulder. Hoole hovered in front of them. It was several minutes before he found the gizzard of the flames. He did not know precisely what he was looking for. One could not come to a fire with preconceived notions and ideas and demand that the flames answer specific questions. That was not how it worked. He had to empty his mind and let the antic flickerings sort themselves into an image. And now in the gizzard of the fire, in that curved yellow plane, was a pinprick of color. Yes! A familiar green was seeping into the yellow. Where had he seen it before? The ember of Hoole had some green in it, but that was not it. And then it burst upon him. *It's the green in the eyes of dire wolves!* The eyes of dire wolves burned like green fire. A certainty glimmered, then grew in Hoole's gizzard: The green of the wolves' eyes bore some trace of magen. If only he could get them to focus the powerful green of their eyes. *Yes . . . yes! That's what we need for an attack on hagsfiends — wolves!* The thought had crossed his mind before, but in truth he hadn't had a clue as to how he would have used the wolves back then. But now he thought he knew. Wolves had cunning strategies and uncanny instincts for what an enemy was about to do. Their unmatched abilities to communicate in the thick of action with nary a sound or detectable signal would be invaluable. But to whom should he go with this plan? Fengo? No. Hordweard. Or as she now called herself, Namara. Yes, Namara MacNamara the brave wolf. The wolf he had believed in when every other wolf and owl thought her a traitor. *I must find Namara*, Hoole thought. *I must run again with the wolves. I must run with Namara!*

CHAPTER SIXTEEN

In Search of a Feather

Yonot fyngrot velink velink,
inhale the vapor and the stink.
Transform this mess of cursed stew
and make it into haggish brew.
Snick, snick the gizzard is nigh on gone
and thus a new monster is spawned.
Gimlich gimloc machten ma,
this is the hagsfiends' nachtga'th.

The smee chant swirled in Kreeth's head as she flew out of the Ice Narrows. She must find a feather from the family of Emerilla. The most likely choice would be Emerilla's father, who had been killed in a battle over the Ice Dagger. She must find the hagsfiend who went off with his head. There was a covey of hagsfiends that lived near the Ice Talons, and one in particular by the name of Penryck interested her. He was a skillful fighter. She had heard that he had thrown in his lot with Lord Arrin. But

Lord Arrin was not faring well these days and Penryck was not one to fly about with losers. She turned east and flew up a twisting channel that penetrated deep into the cliff where it was said there was another ice palace of the old king's, the palace of the Ice Cliffs. Very difficult to find and not nearly as elaborate and grand as the H'rathghar glacier palace, it was said to be deep within an impenetrable maze of ice canyons.

But the Ice Cliffs themselves were riddled with the hollows of hagsfiends. It was a very safe place because the water remained frozen in the channels for most of the year. It was pure daring of King H'rath to have a hideaway so close to hagsfiends. Kreeth had to credit the king and queen for their audacity. But it was also true that most hagsfiends were not extraordinarily bright. It would have been a challenge for them to navigate through the tangled maze of ice channels and canyons. Kreeth, of course, counted herself an exception to this rule.

A hagsfiend now flew in her wake and swooped in beside Kreeth as the narrow channel widened and deepened into a canyon.

"What brings you here, Kreeth?"

"I seek Penryck. He fought in the Battle of the Ice Talons, did he not?"

"Yes, as did I."

Kreeth looked at the hagsfiend but she could not remember her name. "There was an old lieutenant, a Spotted Owl."

"Oh, Strix Hurthwel."

"Who killed him?"

"A hagsfiend named Mycroft."

"And where might this hagsfiend be found?"

"In the Ice Narrows."

"*What?*" Kreeth staggered in flight. "No hagsfiends live in the Narrows except for me."

"He indeed does."

"Don't you 'indeed' me! You, you ..." She wheeled around on her port wing and headed back to the Ice Narrows.

Flying as fast as she could and beating her great ragged wings against the wind, she was in the Narrows before the moon had risen. She had intended to scour every cave and cranny for this Mycroft. But then she suddenly realized there was no need for that. No need at all. The divining eyeball! It had taken years for her to find just the right eyeball, but not long ago she had plucked one from a young Barred Owl who had been blown into the Narrows by accident. It had all happened just before Lutta had hatched.

"Did you bring the feather?" Lutta asked as Kreeth swept into the ice cave.

"No. The head is in the possession of a certain hags-fiend called Mycroft."

Neither Kreeth or Lutta noticed, but the puffowl began to wilf and cower in a corner when the name Mycroft was spoken. He knew of Mycroft, and Mycroft himself had promised to change the puffowl into either an owl or a puffin if he would spy and bring him the secrets of Kreeth's potions. It was a dangerous game the puffowl was playing, but he was sick of Kreeth and her experiments and her abuse. He was sick of being this horrible, ridiculous waddling mixture.

Kreeth got the eyeball and suspended it over a small ice pyramid. It turned slowly and the slivers of gold began to sparkle and glint. An image was forming. "What is it, Auntie?" Lutta asked.

"Shut up. I'm concentrating."

Lutta backed away. Kreeth bent closer to the eyeball.

She saw Mycroft in his cave. He was not an especially large hagsfiend. His tail barely swept the floor. His cave was also strewn with the bits and pieces scavenged from slaughtered creatures. She scanned the cave as he busied himself with his work. Within a minute, no more, she saw it. On an ice ledge in the cave, there was a head — and a handsome one it was! *Well*, she thought, *there is no denying that Spotted Owls are handsome, comely birds*. And this one's eyes had retained a wonderful luster. Kreeth tried to suppress her excitement. She must get a feather or two from that magnificent head and then ... and then she froze.

In an ice bowl on the shelf in Mycroft's cave floated two yarped pellets and the spine of a dead fish. That was her formula! The one she hoped would render water powerless against hagsfiends. There was only one way Mycroft could have come up with that formula! Kreeth spun around. "Puffowl!" she screeched, but the creature was gone.

She flew out of the cave, first turning north into the Narrows and then south. She searched for him for an hour. She went back and looked into her divining eyeball, but it had grown murky and she could see nothing. Where was the cursed little beast? Had he gone to warn Mycroft? There was no way of knowing. At least not until the eyeball had recovered its sight. Until then, she was essentially blind. There could be no divining. Well, she would wait. If there was one thing Kreeth had, it was patience. But it galled her to think that another hagsfiend was living in the Ice Narrows and was now stealing her formulas, her spells! Was there no honor in this world?

And so she waited one night, then two, and finally on

the third night, the divining eyeball cleared. She fully expected to see the puffowl in the cave. She had thought he would have flown to Mycroft's cave to warn him, but the cave appeared empty and the beautiful head was still in its niche. Was it a trap to lure her there? Had the puffowl warned him of her intentions? She looked again in the divining eyeball and muttered an old demonic incantation, a charm especially suited for making visible the invisible and revealing what was concealed. Her breathing calmed. It looked as if neither the puffowl nor Mycroft was around. The time was now.

"Come, Lutta. We need to get you a feather."

CHAPTER SEVENTEEN

The Ice Palace
of the H'rathghar

The splendor of the Ice Palace of the H'rathghar could be seen from many leagues away. It was a majestic sight on a clear sunny day. Its spires of ice shimmered like silver in the blue sky. Its walls and ice bridges and towers all carved by the wind seemed to blaze with a brilliance unmatched by any diamond. But by moonlight it was even more magnificent. As they approached the palace, Theo's mother couldn't stop talking.

"Oh, you've never seen the likes of it. And to think it is all Shadyk's now!"

"But what happened to Lord Arrin?" Theo asked.

"I told you, Theo. He ain't got no respect anymore. Not after the Battle in the Beyond, where he was beat so bad. Half his forces flew off. Some of the hagsfiends left to start up their own bands; one was named Ullryk, I believe."

She believes! She says it so casually. As if it doesn't matter who fights for what anymore. Or who fights on which side. So now they fight among themselves — hagsfiends, rebel owls, kraals. It truly is as Svarr said: A feast for vultures.

Theo's gizzard lurched as he caught sight of the hagsfiends draped over the ice parapets of the palace, their shaggy black wings dark slashes against the shimmering ice. Philma gave four long hoots and then two short, the usual hoot pattern of a Great Horned Owl, but then she paused and gave three more short ones. She swiveled her head toward Theo. "That's our signature call. They know I'm Shadyk's mum. Oh, it's all so grand. You won't believe how fine they treat us, Theo. We're very important now, almost like royalty."

"But how did Shadyk get to be — what do you call him?"

"We'll call him king soon. He's to have a crowning ceremony — what'cha call that?"

"A coronation." *But how did all this happen? Was it raw power on Shadyk's part?* Theo was about to ask when his mother interrupted.

"My goodness, there seem to be more hagsfiends than usual outside the Ice Palace. Oh, and Theo, wait until you see the throne hollow and Shadyk sitting on the throne. To think, a son of mine sitting upon the H'rathian throne. Ain't it grand?"

A sickening feeling swept through Theo as they entered the palace and proceeded to the throne room. It was immediately evident why the hagsfiends were all outside. The inside of the once magnificent palace was rotting. *Rotten ice!* The two words shrieked in Theo's brain. He had always thought it was just an expression, but now he knew that it was real. Inside the palace the ice was cloudy, and it looked as if it were disintegrating. Theo had seen a honeycomb in a tree hollow in the S'yrthghar and that was exactly what this ice looked like to him, a honeycomb. *Sweet rotten ice!,* Theo thought as they entered the throne hollow. The palace was rotting from the inside, so only the outer walls were safe for the hagsfiends to perch on. How long would they remain to serve their leader, their monarch, this ridiculous-looking owl who perched upon the melting throne? Shadyk was not that much larger than when Theo had left, and his feathers were bedraggled and looked as if they had not been preened in ages, although four female owls, a Pygmy Owl and three Elf Owls, were busy running their beaks through his feathers and picking nits from his ear slits and between his talons.

"Mum?" Shadyk leaned forward.

"Yes, sweetie. Look who I've brought."

Shadyk immediately stiffened. "How often do I have to tell you that I am to be addressed as Commander — Commander Strong Talon." He turned to Theo. "Good evening, brother. It has been a long time. You have been studying, I suppose, not soldiering." He turned to the other owls who were in the hollow. "My brother, Theo, is of a studious bent. Not a fighting sort of owl." There were mumbles that Theo interpreted as disapproving. "Indeed," Shadyk flew down from the throne, that fabled throne that was said to have been miraculously sculpted by the elements to resemble a tree with scores of limbs on which the king, his queen, princes, and princesses could all perch. But most of the limbs had rotted away, and it was evident that all this once resplendent throne could now sustain was the weight of one rather small Great Horned and his minions of tiny Elf and Pygmy owls. Theo stepped forward.

"That's far enough!" Shadyk flapped his wings.

"Good evening." Theo paused, and Shadyk swelled up into a threat posture. "Commander Strong Talon," Theo added.

In those brief seconds, Theo realized that Shadyk had either forgotten or denied their past history — all the times that he had protected his younger brother from his father's rages, nursed not only his bruised feelings but his bruised wings and broken shafts — it was in that moment that Theo realized that Shadyk was not just yoicks but completely insane. A mad glint danced in his amber eyes.

"Ain't it all so grand, Theo?" Philma whispered to him. He thought that if his mum said "grand" one more time he'd yarp a pellet. "He's got quite a way about him, don't he, lovey?"

"My family and I shall adjourn to the banquet hollow." Shadyk turned to the Elf and Pygmy owls. "Please join us, my sweets." The small owls twittered about him, making fawning gestures.

The banquet hollow was a disgusting mess. The remains of half-eaten lemmings, snow squirrels, and ice rats were strewn around but no one seemed to notice or care. The melting ice was streaked with blood. Theo had thought he was hungry but had no appetite now, even as several owls flew in with fresh kill.

"So, brother," Shadyk swiveled his head toward Theo. "Still studying? Join the Glauxian Brothers yet?" he drawled, and cast a glance at his audience. There was a loud raucous churring from the delegation of owls who had followed them into the dining hollow. They clearly had contempt for study and contemplative owls.

"Uh . . ." Theo hesitated. "Yes, um, yes, I have been studying and am thinking of taking my vows." *So far, the truth. They need not know that I have taken vows as a Guardian on a faraway island in the S'yrthghar and sworn allegiance to the rightful heir to this throne.* For the first time in his life when not in the midst of the violence of war and given no choice, Theo felt true rage rising within him. *Now,* he thought, *I am truly a warrior!*

"I don't know if many of us in this palace have the time for such study. It does seem rather like a luxury now, does it not?" Shadyk drawled while weaving and bobbing his head about to catch everyone's eye except that of his brother.

His ways have become very strange, Theo thought. *He speaks in an odd manner, each word prolonged to the point of silliness. And he casts his eyes in glances that are both simpering and haughty. My brother is mad. And yet no one sees it. Not Mum, not Wyg. Not the four little owls flitting about him. How has he done this? How has he gathered these owls and these hagsfiends around him? Does no one else see that this palace is rotting? Are the only sane creatures the hagsfiends who perch on the parapets and the turrets?*

At that moment, he saw a Spotted Owl come to serve her master a plump ice rat. She approached him in mincing steps, her head bent, obsequious, submissive, the perfect attendant to a king on the rotting throne. But despite that bowed head, Theo glimpsed a glint of gold in her dark brown eyes, her very sane dark brown eyes, and he knew that he was the only one who recognized her sanity. And who also recognized *her*: This was Emerilla, daughter of Strix Strumajen and Strix Hurthwel!

CHAPTER EIGHTEEN
To Be Emerilla

Delicately, Kreeth wove the feather into Lutta's plumage. "You see, my dear, it is not enough to look like just any Spotted Owl. You must be a particular one. With this feather from the head of Emerilla's father you will be able, in a sense, to become her. Yes, you have mastered the call of the Spotted Owls, the long *whuff-whuff.* And you are excellent at capturing that peculiar tilting action of their plummels as they go into a banking turn, and you even think like a Spotted Owl. But now you must think like Emerilla. Because, as your half-hags heard, this new king from the strange tree in the south is searching for her. You are vital to my plan to get the ember. If you can become Emerilla, the ember is mine!

"Now listen and learn, Lutta. Hagsfiends do not really have what owls call a "true gizzard," but with this feather, well . . . you will get close to having one. Owl gizzards are strange. They serve no good purpose. It is much better to have a hagsfiend's gizzard. It is a simple organ that digests food and does not bother us with the so-called finer sensibilities and emotions."

"What are emotions exactly?" Lutta asked.

"Silly feelings that get in the way of actions." She paused and fixed Lutta with a beady-eyed stare. "And this will be the most difficult part of your mission. You must act like an owl with a gizzard, but at the same time you must resist the instincts with which a gizzard might distract you. A gizzard could prove dangerous! Do you understand?"

"Yes, Auntie."

"In this mission, there is simply no room for emotions. You must do nothing that would jeopardize the mission."

"No, never! Never!" Lutta felt a strange twinge in her belly. Something squirmed deep within her. She had experienced the first turnings of gizzard, not a true owl gizzard, but nonetheless it was a queer feeling. A sensation that she did not completely dislike. In fact, it was a sensation that made her feel more . . . more . . . She searched for the words: more complete.

Her mission was to fly to this island in the south and steal the ember, the Ember of Hoole. She must not let this so-called gizzard distract her.

When Kreeth had first heard about the ember and the great tree ruled by this idiot who wanted to rid the owl world of all magic, she had started to devise her strategy. She had, thanks to Lutta's half-hags' reconnaissance flight, heard the facts. But she realized that what she needed was not more information but knowledge of a deeper sort. She needed to know the nature of this owl named Hoole who was in possession of the most powerful magic in the world, yet wanted to rid the world of it. She plucked a withered gizzard from her collection, which hung on ice picks. Placing it in a solution, she began to mumble peculiar words. It was a dream-sight divination that had to be spoken both forward and backward without a single mistake — "Veeblyn spyn crynik spyn veeblyn Hoole Elooh nylbeev nyps kinyrc nyps nylbeev."

It took her three tries, but she finally succeeded. She could now enter the dreams of Hoole. Not every dream, and not all the time. Some dreams would prove useless and give no insight into his nature. But others would be quite valuable. For several days as she slept, she was stirred by the dreams of Hoole, but they were, for the most part, unremarkable. The usual ones: a succulent prey that slipped through one's talons, flying the starry configurations of a night sky to suddenly find it daytime and a mob of crows closing in. There were a few dreams of the Battle in the Beyond, but not as many as she would have liked. These battle dreams yielded a wealth of information about

Hoole's fighting strategies, and she was intrigued by the strange devices that he and three other owls wore on their talons, which extended them into fearsomely sharp weapons. But then one day, late in the afternoon just before her usual time to rise, she entered a dream that she knew was crucial to her understanding of Hoole and the success of the mission.

Kreeth found herself flying through thick fog that was beginning to thin. It seemed that shimmering stars were suspended in the pearly mist. But they were not stars at all. They were the white dots of a Spotted Owl. Hoole was dreaming of the owl Emerilla for whom they were searching. Nothing unusual about that. She had known that the Spotted Owl was the object of their search. But though Kreeth herself had no owl's gizzard, she could see that Hoole's gizzard was in turmoil. He was drawn to this owl, concerned for her safety, fascinated by her courage.

Kreeth snapped awake. "It makes our task so easy!" she exclaimed.

Kreeth stepped to the sleeping Lutta and patted the feather she had earlier woven into her primaries.

"Now, my Lutta," she whispered. "You will truly become Emerilla. Don't you feel it?"

Lutta did begin to feel different, but then again she was not sure what it was she was feeling. More than anything, Lutta was confused, but she dared not ask any more questions because Kreeth was in a highly agitated state, and when she got this way it was not a good idea to pester her. Still, Lutta wondered what exactly she was — Hagsfiend? Owl? Snowy? Spotted, Pygmy, Elf? Or Great Horned, as she had appeared soon after she hatched? She sometimes felt split up into a hundred different pieces. Yes, it could be confusing — and very lonely.

CHAPTER NINETEEN

An Old Friend

In the northern part of the S'yrthghar, winter weather had set in and the night was aslant with a slashing wind of sleet and snow and rain. The wintry weather reminded Hoole of the dwindling number of nights to Short Light and this made him fly all the faster. Every night the darkness lengthened and the sun grew weaker, staggering up over the horizon like some crippled sky creature until finally there would come that morning when it would not appear at all. That would be the Long Night when they must strike.

Hoole flew alone on a northeasterly course. He was unfamiliar with sleet. In the N'yrthghar, it was so cold and dry, there was no sleet, only snow.

"Great Glaux, I'll wear out my wings flying through this slop," he muttered as he approached Broken Talon Point. Phineas and the Snow Rose had protested when he said that they must go back to the great tree to report what they had found so far. The Pygmy and the Snowy had wanted to accompany him, and it took a lot of arguing on Hoole's part to convince them that he would be quite safe. "It's more important for you to fly back and share what we have found and to seek out more Rogue smiths who are willing to be slipgizzles." Finally, they had relented.

The images in the fire had shown Namara — the wolf once called Hordweard — in the harsh and inhospitable region northeast of Broken Talon Point, not in the Beyond where the dire wolves had lived ever since Fengo had led them there. It did not surprise Hoole that Namara had chosen to leave the Beyond. She had lived most of her life there as one of several mates of the demonic wolf called MacHeath. But she had left her clan and shown great courage and endurance in hunting down the traitorous MacHeath and warning Hoole of Lord Arrin's approach before the Battle in the Beyond. Had it not been for Namara, they would have never been prepared for the attack. Ever since that day she had been regarded as a hero by all the wolves of the Beyond. But hero or not, Namara wanted no part of their society. In her time alone tracking down her old mate, she had become strong again, and confident and beautiful. She had declared that her name was no longer Hordweard but Namara. "I am Namara now. My clan is MacNamara. I am a clan unto myself." Hoole needed her now and was determined to find her.

He knew the way of the wolves. He had lived in Fengo's cave, breathing the air that the wolves breathed and smelling their scent marks. But his education was not complete until he had joined a byrrgis, the traveling formation of wolves, and hunted with them. And although he had not become a wolf in his shape or body, he had in his mind. His beak had felt like fangs, his feathers like fur. It was almost as if he could read the wolves as he read the flames.

Those feelings were returning. He knew he was drawing close to Namara. He could feel her hunting nearby — was it a stray caribou? A bobcat? With each beat of his wing, he felt himself becoming more wolf than bird. A confounding but thrilling paradox.

He spotted her just as the moon was sliding down toward the horizon into another night in another world, and the first gray of dawn began to peel away the darkness. It was a winter-thin caribou she was tracking. Hoole settled in a tree to watch the ritual of lochinvyrr that was about to be enacted. He dared not interrupt it. An agreement was being made between predator and prey. The prey, in a silent language, said, "My meat is valuable, my meat will sustain you. I am worthy." It was not a moment of victory or defeat but one of dignity.

When Namara had finished with the kill, Hoole swept down from the tree. She lifted her blood-soaked muzzle.

"Hoole, dear Hoole!" How odd those soft words seemed coming from that blood-drenched face. "What brings you here, young'un? Oh, forgive me — you are now king."

"No, I shall always be just Hoole. I care not for such titles."

Namara laughed softly. "What brings you here to this lonely place?"

"Is it lonely for you, Namara?" Hoole asked.

"No, not really, and if it were, it would be a loneliness of my own choosing. You know me, Hoole. But tell me, why have you come?"

Hoole told her of his encounter with the hagsfiend in Ambala and how he had suspected that others were around. "So I went to the fire to read the flames."

Namara nodded her head as she gnawed on the caribou. "Yes, you were a flame reader. I remember now. And the flames told you that there were hagsfiends loose in the S'yrthghar."

"In the Desert of Kuneer to be exact. A perfect place for them, of course. But it told me even more."

"What was that?" Namara lifted her head. Her tilted green eyes sparkled. Hoole leaned forward into their green light. He knew he was right. This was the light he had seen in the flames.

"Namara, the green light in the eyes of wolves will

destroy the fyngrot. I know this. I know it through the flames. I know it in my gizzard." He paused before going on. He was frightened of asking the next question but he must. "Namara, I need you to lead a wolf pack into the Desert of Kuneer. You are a loner, I know, but you are a natural leader, too. The wolves of the Beyond hold you in great esteem. I am not asking you to live with them. I am asking you to lead them. This is a battle for the wolves. I will go with you. I shall fight. In the Battle of the Beyond I learned from my mother to resist the fyngrot, but I cannot destroy it. My family's palace, the Ice Palace of the N'yrthghar, has fallen into enemy hands. And now, in the S'yrthghar, there are hagsfiends. Before I can go north again and lead my owls of the great tree on to the H'rathghar glacier to oust those outlaws and tyrants, I must make sure the S'yrthghar is rid of the hagsfiends."

"And once this is done, this business with the hags-fiends, will you fly straightaway to the N'yrthghar?"

"No, not straightaway. There is much to be done before we are ready for that war."

"And what is that?" Somehow things had turned around. Namara was not answering Hoole's questions but asking the questions. Hoole felt it was important to answer her questions with great care and thought. *This, in some way, is a test*, he thought.

"There is much to be done before the Guardians of the Great Ga'Hoole Tree are ready. We had one success at the Battle in the Beyond, and though it wasn't mere chance, we must be better prepared next time. Only four of us fought with battle claws then. That was all we had. We must make more and teach others how to fly with them. We need more colliers, more owls to learn the art of smithing who can produce the battle claws because we have few ice weapons in our part of the world and they are difficult to keep. And —" Hoole paused and looked deeply into the tilting green eyes of Namara "— we need to learn to think like wolves."

Namara seemed to relax now. "This is good, my friend. You are right. You must teach them the way of the byrrgis. And if it is colliers and smiths that you need, well, there are more each day. They are learning quickly how to pick up coals, not from the mouth of the volcanoes as you did, mind you, but the ones that are flung down to the base. And now I even see them heading out for forest fires."

"Really?" Hoole was amazed.

Namara nodded and continued, "There is even a smith with a forge near here. They are all very devoted to you, Hoole, and I think they would not hesitate to help."

"And yourself, Namara, will you help?"

"Of course, dear friend. It is the least I can do for the

only creature on earth who believed in me and knew I was not a traitor. We can set out for the Beyond at First Black, as you owls call it. Fengo will help me raise the pack. Don't worry. Now help yourself to some of this caribou."

"Oh, no. It is a scrawny thing. You eat the rest. I'm sure there are rats and voles scrambling around here someplace."

"As you like, Hoole, as you like. But come share my den when you have fed. It is right over there by that old scrub oak. I've made a burrow at its roots. It will do fine for a wolf and a Spotted Owl."

That day, well fed, the owl and the wolf shared a den.

Hoole hadn't dreamed of the lovely Spotted Owl since that first time. It seemed as if each time he nearly entered a dream about her, something would drag him from it, and so his days remained dreamless.

CHAPTER TWENTY

A Rotting Palace

In another part of the owl world, the Spotted Owl of whom Hoole had once dreamed, Emerilla, spoke in a hushed voice to the Great Horned Owl Theo. The two had met in the most unlikely place: the Ice Palace of the H'rathghar.

"Hush! Don't call me Emerilla. Here I am known as Sigrid," she said.

Theo had taken his leave of the banquet hollow and his brother's company as soon as he could without arousing suspicion.

"But you are she, aren't you?" Theo cocked his head.

"Yes, but how did you know?"

Theo thought for a minute. How did he know? It was just a feeling in his gizzard. It was not so much that she looked like her mother, Strix Strumajen, but that she seemed different from all the other owls in the Ice Palace. "I just knew."

This seemed to satisfy Emerilla. "Do you know where my mother is?"

"With Hoole," Theo whispered.

"And you, too, you live there as well?"

"Yes." The two owls spoke in fragments, half sentences with nods and blinks, daring not to say anything that could give them away. It was amazing how much information they conveyed in such a brief time. Emerilla had been working in the Ice Palace since it had fallen to Shadyk. Luckily, no one had recognized her because the battles she had fought in had, for the most part, been skirmishes in a region far from where Shadyk and his troops had been fighting. There were apparently skirmishes, fights, battles, and clashes raging all over the Northern Kingdoms. It was no longer simply a two-sided war. It was also Lord Arrin's soldiers against Lord Unser's near the Bitter Sea where there had never been fighting before. It was sometimes hagsfiends against hagsfiends. "Are any of H'rath's old troops fighting with these owls?" Theo asked.

"There might be a few, but if they are, none of them are fighting for the kingdom as it once was."

"What do you mean?"

"The really loyal ones went south to the S'yrthghar. The ones left have forgotten everything the H'rathian dynasty flew for. There are factions, but really it is each owl for himself." Emerilla paused, leaned forward, and whispered, "The Ice Palace is rotting from the inside because every code of honor has been violated. There is no H'rathian code here. It has been destroyed. And so the ice melts! It was foretold in ancient prophecies of H'rathmore."

Then once again, Theo heard the same words that Svarr had spoken: "This place and the entire N'yrthghar is a feast for vultures."

Theo took to heart what Emerilla had been telling him, but still something did not seem quite right in her explanation. *If it is just a matter of time before the hagsfiends leave and the palace can be taken, why wait to join her mother at the island?* Theo wondered. She was holding something back.

"Why delay? Why not leave now? You know so much about the palace. Your information would be invaluable." She blinked nervously at him. "What is it, Sigrid? You are not telling me everything."

She shut her eyes tightly for more than a blink and then opened them and looked straight at Theo. "I am a close fighter."

"I had heard that from your mother," Theo replied.

"There is no owl better than myself with a close blade."

"Yes, go on." Theo nodded.

"Shadyk is your brother."

It was not a question, it was a statement. Theo felt his gizzard clinch.

"I plan to assassinate him."

Theo inhaled deeply. His gizzard quaked.

"He is insane, Theo. He tortures owls for the fun of it. He sits on that rotting throne and dreams of an owl universe. Do you know that it was he who killed your father?"

Theo gasped.

"He tried to kill your sister, the gadfeather, too. He will probably try to kill you as well. You need to get out of here quickly. When he has one of the fits, he has even tried to kill his own guards."

"How can my mother not see this?"

"He controls himself when she is around. And she treats him like a chick. She is blind to any of his faults." She paused. "In his own way, he is worse than any hagsfiend, and I shall kill him when the time is right." She paused again. "You must get out. Get out immediately."

But Theo resolved to stay a bit longer. He would be vigilant and take care, but he wanted to see more of the Ice Palace. He wanted to be able to send back as much information as possible to Hoole, and he was not sure if they should wait until the hagsfiends left the palace. If all of these factions were fighting in the N'yrthghar, it might be too late. Another faction might take over. And the Ice Palace was rotting, decomposing as they spoke.

Theo returned to the banquet hollow. It did not appear that he was missed. His mother was excited. "Oh, Theo, your dear brother is offering us the most splendid quarters for the day. The ice hollows in the eastern parapet."

Shadyk churred and an odd light danced in his amber eyes. He cocked his head. "I am sure, dear brother, you will be most comfortable there. Pleasant dreams."

Is my mother completely benighted? And what about Wyg? He as well? Theo looked about the niche in the eastern defense wall. Even here on an outer wall exposed to the cold, the interior of this sleeping hollow had begun to show signs of rot. He could even hear the ice worms stirring. "Mum, Wyg?"

"Yes, dear."

"Don't you hear the ice worms stirring?"

"Oh, it's just your imagination, Theo. You were always so sensitive."

Am I going mad? How can they not see this?

"You know, Theo, this is where they said the egg of the young prince was first set down by Queen Siv. What an honor indeed to be allowed to sleep here. And just look at the gleam of these walls — like silver. And see? Even the morning stars shine through."

The walls are melting! Theo nearly screamed. He felt as if the universe was being turned inside out or upside down — or both. "Wyg," he said in a gentle quiet voice. "Do you think that there is something wrong with the ice? Doesn't it seem rather ... rather ..." — he did not want to use the word "rotten" — "rather unstable?"

"Just a bit, Theo, but come Short Light, it will be solid again."

"Oh, Theo, you must stay for Long Night. Your brother has planned such a wonderful celebration. And it is less than a moon cycle away."

Long Night was one of the most festive holidays in the N'yrthghar, for it celebrated the disappearance of the sun and the longest darkness. In the world of owls night was always more valued than day. At Long Night, both young and older owls could fly to their gizzards' content and waste little time on sleep. There were all sorts of sports and games, and gadfeathers came to sing and do their lively sky jigs in front of the bright plate of moon.

But Long Night with a mad brother? Theo thought. *Horrible. And yet if I stay I would be the most valuable slipgizzle in all the N'yrthghar.*

CHAPTER TWENTY-ONE

Desert Hags

From the air the byrrgis looked like a long silvery streak coursing through the countryside. Hoole had never imagined that such a gathering of wolves could be mustered. But after her long absence from the Beyond, Namara was greeted like a returning hero. The clan chieftains ran in the forefront of the byrrgis. There was stalwart Dunmore, fearless Duncan MacDuncan, rugged Stormfast, dauntless Banquo, and behind them scores of others from various clans. Fengo himself, though old, was also part of this byrrgis. Although Hoole was the king of the great tree, the wolves knew that the young king was indeed a guardian of all creatures, be they of land or sky. They remembered him from the time he had run with them on the hunt and how when he killed he performed the lochinvyrr as if he were a wolf. They remembered his courage in battle and, perhaps most of all, they remembered his loyalty to Hordweard, the outcast wolf, who now, as Namara MacNamara, led this byrrgis.

The forests were vanishing as Hoole looked below at the ground turning scrubby with brambles and low-growing, shallow-rooted plants. They were nearing the Desert of Kuneer. Traveling both day and night, they had made good time. Hoole had seen no signs of crows, and in any case did not fear daylight flying now, for with the wolves directly beneath him he could quickly dive into the byrrgis for protection if crows began to mob.

Together, the wolves and Hoole had devised a plan. They would not travel too far into the desert, but first look for a good base, either a cave or sand embankment that they could burrow into or hide behind. Hoole and the wolves would work together. Because of his aerial vantage point, Hoole was responsible for scanning the terrain for a base of operations. The wolves, given their keen sense of smell, would send out a tracking team to find the hagsfiends or any telltale signs of them, such as the tumbledown that Phineas had found.

It was not long before Hoole spotted the perfect hide-out; a large cave in the side of a low sandstone shelf with some outlying rocks. As soon as they had settled into this natural fortification, Hoole took command. Perched on one of the rocks, he looked around.

"My thought is that this place, so perfect for us, would also offer protection to the hagsfiends. We found it quickly. I think that there are similar formations that might give them shelter. My plan is to fly out at dawn and reconnoiter. The hagsfiends will be asleep."

"But what about the crows, Hoole?" Fengo asked.

"The desert does not seem their kind of territory."

"'Seem,' Hoole?" Fengo asked. There was a low grumbling among the wolves. "I think you should fly with a guard."

"I'll go!" "Count me in!" "Me as well." A dozen wolves called out to accompany the young king.

"I am sure," Hoole said, "that three will be enough." He scanned the pack. "Donneghail, Cailean, and Camran, you will run with me." The three wolves were among the largest of the entire pack. They would defend him well. Donneghail, in addition to being fast and strong, was alert to the smallest things. If there was tumbledown in the brush, Donneghail would spot it.

Following sunrise, Hoole had not been flying long when he saw a depression in the sand with big boulders along one side. He slowed his flight and then spiraled down to alert the three wolves.

"Donneghail, you go out ahead and see if you spot any of the tumbledown. Remember it is not as black as their flight feathers — just soft balls of gray fluff."

"Yes, Hoole."

When he came back, he reported that there were no such telltale signs, neither tumbledown nor hag scent.

Hoole lofted himself once more into flight, and the three wolves loped along beneath him. *Perhaps*, Hoole thought, *these hideouts are not as plentiful as I thought.* But at just that moment, he saw the wolves suddenly stop below him, and then about a quarter league ahead, he saw them, their immense black shapes billowing in a sandpit. Hoole flew a little closer for a better look. Even though they were only about twice the size of owls, their wings were huge and it appeared as if the darkest storm clouds had settled on the earth. There must have been at least thirty of them, their black-feathered bodies rising and falling in the rhythms of sleep. Hoole carved a turn and flew back to a boulder where the three wolves waited.

"There are at least thirty of them."

"The sun is high. So there are hours left until they rouse themselves," Cailean said. "Should we go back and get the others and then attack them?"

"Sounds like a good idea," Donneghail said. Camran agreed.

"But, my friends, there is a problem." Hoole spoke thoughtfully. "We would have the element of surprise, but the brightness of the day would rob the greenness of your eyes' light."

Hoole had thought about this deeply since he had first looked into the flames of Rupert's fire and had seen the green light that had so reminded him of the ember. It had come to him at that time that Grank himself had told him long ago that he had first seen the image of the ember in the eyes of Fengo. Hoole, most of all, was suspicious of the power of the ember in many ways. He had seen evidence of how it could alter those who came near it. Was it its light, its heat, that caused these altered states? And was there an affinity between some of the ember's powers and that of wolves? They both shared this intense green light. Was it possible that the wolves had a power equal to — if not greater than — that of the fyngrot of the hagsfiends? How then might it be used to greater effect?

"We must have the darkness of the night for my plan to work," Hoole said.

"Aaah!" All three wolves realized at once that what the young king said was true. Hoole had explained to them that the green light in the eyes of the wolves was so similar to that of the ember, he felt in his gizzard that it could shatter the fyngrot. They must trade the element of surprise for the effectiveness of the dark. And this would be a perfect night because the moon had dwenked and the newing had not yet begun. It would be black as pitch.

*   *   *

"There are at least thirty of them," Hoole explained when they returned to the other wolves. "They sleep in a shallow pit. Much shallower than this one. My plan is this." Hoole lofted down from the rock where he had perched and dragged one talon through the sand. "This is the shape of the pit. There are rocks here, here, here, here, and here. That is five rocks with broad surfaces. There are thirty of you as well. You will divide into five teams, six wolves to a team, and I shall help out wherever needed.

"We need to leave before tween time." Hoole paused. "Sorry, I forget myself. That is owl talk for the time between the last drop of daylight and the first shadows of night. We'll approach the rocks under the camouflage of these first shadows. Now, do you all understand the strategy?"

"Yes," they answered. It was a strategy that was very similar to the one they used in hunting caribou.

"Remember, if we do this right, there should be very little fighting at the onset, and then you can set in for the kill."

Once again the wolves bayed, "Yes."

"Fengo, you are prepared to lead the howls?"

"Yes, Hoole. We will start with the lowest of the howls, the close-to-ground whines, proceed to the pack howl, and then to the death howl."

"To the death howl!" Stormfast, a huge wolf leaped up on his hind legs and struck at the sinking sun with his forepaws.

"To the death howl!" The others leaped toward the sky.

Hoole marveled. There was nothing more faithful than a wolf. So noble and so intelligent.

And although the ember was far away, smoldering in its teardrop strongbox, he felt the power of it every time he looked into the green fire of those wolf eyes. Even though Grank had told Hoole that he had first glimpsed the image of the ember in the eyes of Fengo, in truth, every wolf seemed to have a reflection of this ember in their eyes, that unearthly green shimmer that inspired Hoole. He did not need to have the ember close by. He only needed to look into a wolf's eyes. It would be this same green that emanated from those eyes that Hoole knew deep in his gizzard would lead to the downfall of the hagsfiends. But it was a magic they did not understand, could never believe in.

CHAPTER TWENTY-TWO
The Night of the Green Light

Ever since Hoole had run with the wolves that first time in the Beyond, there had been fleeting moments when he felt more wolf than owl. It was like that now as Hoole flew low over their silver-and-gray backs. The owl and the wolves were moving forward with the shadows as the night came on. Hoole felt each light footfall of the wolves. His breath came in the same panting rhythms. The wolves had assumed the tight pack of an ambush byrrgis. There would be a subtle shifting of positions as they advanced. It was the seamless movements, their flawless communication that was the real force that drove their intricate strategies, whether it was for hunting, tracking, or simply traveling; Hoole found it fascinating. The wolves played out these designs through a series of silent signals that appeared as smooth as the orbits of planets or the transit of the stars across the sky. The wolves had a name for such strategies: They called them the Great Game.

The night was growing darker. There would be no moon, and shortly the hagsfiends would begin to stir. But as each minute passed, Hoole felt himself grow more wolflike. He felt the dish shape of his face begin to extend into the night and could imagine the almost square muzzle of a wolf instead of a beak. His ear slits seemed to move toward the top of his head, and he could twitch them in one direction and then another to collect sounds. In his chest, he felt a bigger heart pumping loudly, and even his talons began to feel different. *I am not a wolf, but I am a wolf,* he thought. *A winged wolf.*

They were now approaching the five boulders. They would hunker down behind them and then when the first hags began to stir, Hoole would give a signal and the Great Game would enter the next phase.

They waited and waited. Finally, Hoole detected a change in the hags' breathing. He dragged his talon across a rock's surface. The scratching of the talon was the first signal, and the wolves leaped to their positions on the boulders. Led by Fengo, the howling began, a wild and untamed sound scrolling through the night. The hagsfiends were aghast. They staggered from their sleep and in a great confusion tried to rise and loft themselves into the air. But the night was now crisscrossed with a shimmering green light. Hoole could hear the hagsfiends giving commands to their half-hags in that peculiar language reserved only for speaking to the tiny poisonous creatures. Although he could see their plumage stirring, the half-hags did not emerge. It was as if the green light had made them fall yeep before they could even fly out from the safety of their hosts' feathers. This sent the hagsfiends into a panic. An order to cast a fyngrot was shrieked. Hoole knew that this would be the real test.

The wolves now tipped their heads up. Green light issued from thirty pairs of eyes. Fengo began howling commands to direct their gaze, and just as he had hoped, shimmering green light beams shot across and over the hagsfiends as they tried to cast their ghastly fyngrot. Glaring yellow flashed from haggish eyes, but green blades of light cut through it, and the yellow fractured, shattering into millions of pieces.

Hoole, aloft, together with Fengo on the boulder coordinated their commands from their different vantage points and guided the wolves' eyes. For those hagsfiends who had lofted themselves into flight, it was as if the entire night had turned into a slope glazed in slippery green ice. They were losing their purchase on the air. Then Hoole saw something that froze his gizzard. "Behind you, Fengo! Behind!"

Two hagsfiends who had slid down from the night sky

were slithering on their bellies through the desert sand. Their talons were inches from Fengo's back. Suddenly there were streaks of blood in the silver fur, and Fengo was rising in the night, clutched in the immense talons of a hagsfiend.

"Look up! Look up! Cast your green!" Hoole shouted, but his words were swallowed by the night. The second hagsfiend was now racing toward Fengo's head. One talon extended beyond the length of the rest. The truth of this moment began to sink in. The hagsfiend was going for Fengo's eyes. Blood spurted into the night. A sickening feeling engulfed him.

When Hoole had fought in the Battle of the Beyond, he had not been aware that his mother had sustained a direct hit. He thought she was beside him the entire time until he suddenly became aware that she was gone. This time, however, he had seen the attack. This time he could do something and a rage built in Hoole's gizzard. He had never felt anything so intensely in his life. It was as if the heat of the ember was rising within him. A passion that seemed almost craven in its power flooded his entire being. He flew directly at the hagsfiend that had seized Fengo. They were high in the air. If the hag dropped Fengo, the wolf would surely die. And Hoole — not even half of the size of a hag — would not have the strength to carry his weight.

"Do not drop him. I command you to set him down

gently!" The words sounded entirely foolish. It was hard to imagine, let alone daring, to command a hagsfiend to do such a thing. But if any creature had looked up, they would have seen a curious sight. Overhead, an owl began to glow luminous green. He appeared to be composed more of light than feathers and bones and flesh. The hagsfiend was trying desperately to cast a fyngrot, but the yellow simply washed away in the night. "Down, down gently! Gently." The hag, as if in some strange hypnotic state, began to sink slowly through the air and gently laid the bleeding wolf on the boulder.

Taking their cue from Hoole, the other wolves began to bring the rest of the hagsfiends to ground by manipulating the beams of their eyes until a large web of green light was formed that, like a spider gathering its prey, drew them in.

Then, when the hagsfiends touched ground, a silent signal was given, and the wolves sank their teeth into the throats of the stupefied hagsfiends. Hoole ripped open the chest of the hag that had gouged out Fengo's eye, and another wolf killed the hag whose talons had clutched Fengo.

Blood seeped from Fengo's empty eye socket. The other eye still burned fiercely, but Fengo's breath came in ragged gasps. "My time on earth is near its end, my friend, dear Hoole."

"No! No! It cannot be. It simply cannot be!"

"But it is, Hoole," Fengo said calmly.

"The ember. I felt the power of the ember. It brought the hagsfiends to the ground. It can bring you back to life."

"No, no, young king. It does not work that way."

"The magic of the ember can, though. It is good magen, not nachtmagen."

"Just the point, young'un. Good magic works in harmony with Lupus and Glaux and nature. Death is also part of the Great Game we wolves play. I am an old wolf, my time has come. You must not go against such things just because you have the ember." There was a weird gurgling sound that came from Fengo as his chest heaved, gasping for every breath. "Say farewell to my old friend Grank.... And now the time." With his last bit of strength, he cocked his head and fixed his single eye on Hoole. It was time for lochinvyrr. Even though Hoole had not brought on this death, and although Fengo was not Hoole's prey, this was an honorable death. It must be recognized as such in order for Fengo's spirit to climb the spirit trail of the stars to the cave of souls, the wolf heaven.

Namara, who had been standing off to one side, now approached Hoole. "The hagsfiends are all dead, Hoole. There were thirty to start with and there are thirty bodies accounted for."

Hoole looked up. He saw small piles of feathers. Once again, as in Ambala, he was astonished at how small they appeared in death. Hoole wondered, however, if these were the only hagsfiends in the S'yrthghar. And if they had simply strayed here after the Battle in the Beyond or if they had been ordered here by Lord Arrin. Had they diminished the enemy's strength enough so that when the Short Light came, the enemy could be defeated? Well, he had done his best with the help of the wolves, but there were many questions still to be answered, and at least one battle yet to be fought.

And was the world of owls any closer to being rid of all magic? That was the real question.

The wolves dragged Fengo's body far from those of the hagsfiends. At the bottom of a sandy rise they dug a pit and buried their chief so the carrion eaters would not tear his body to pieces.

The owl and the wolves then left the desert, and before the night was half over they were back in Ambala where they found a large old oak. It had turned cold and the wolves made what they called a sleep fold, in which they huddled together for warmth when there was no real shelter. As for Hoole, he was happy to be back in a tree. The night was still too young for any self-respecting owl to sleep, so he flew to the topmost branch of the tree. The darkness flowed with stars. Grank had taught him the names of the different stars and constellations, and Hoole knew that the group of stars that the owls called the Golden Talons was known as Lupus or the Star Wolf to the wolves. And as the last stars climbed to the front paws of the wolf, Hoole felt a strange mixture of sadness and joy: sadness at the loss of his old friend, and joy as he watched the spirit trail burn out of the night sky just beneath the Star Wolf. *He's on his way to the cave of souls*, Hoole thought. Quietly, Hoole lifted off from the tree and flew into the night.

Am I flying or loping through these stars? he thought as he traced with a wing tip the outline of the Star Wolf's muzzle. There was a gathering of mist in the shape of a wolf that appeared to trot softly up the spirit trail. It passed Hoole and then paused. Turning its head, it raised its muzzle high and a sonorous howl flowed that was made of clouds and mists, star shine, and all the heavenly bits of the night. "Good-bye, my friend," Hoole whispered. "Good-bye."

And far away on an island in the middle of the southern sea, another Spotted Owl peered into his own fire and saw that his old friend from the Beyond was climbing the spirit trail to the cave of souls. *Glaumora? The cave of souls?* thought Grank. *They are one. We shall meet again.*

CHAPTER TWENTY-THREE

Emerilla?

The great tree shook violently in the early winter storm. "Only a fool would be out there tonight," Justin, a young Short-eared Owl, said. "What in Glaux's name are Grank and Strix Strumajen perched on the lookout for?"

"They ain't fools, Justin. I just come off watch, and we think we spotted her daughter flying in."

"The young master of the short blade, eh? Well, stars in glaumora — that'll set the old Strix up something fine, wouldn't it?"

"It certainly would."

Now both owls became curious enough that they crept from the coziness of the guard hollow they shared near the very top of the great tree and peered up. A lovely Spotted Owl had just landed next to Strix Strumajen and Grank.

"Mum?"

"Emerilla!" Strix Strumajen's beak dropped open.

"This is your daughter?" Grank asked.

"Yes!" Strix Strumajen gasped and then folded her daughter gently into her wings. The young Spotted Owl closed her eyes tight and tried not to fall off the branch as a wave of nausea swept through her. *Don't yarp, don't yarp. It must be that thing they call a gizzard. Emotions don't just get in the way,* she thought. *They make you sick.*

"Are you all right, dear? You look a bit shaky."

"Fine, Mum. Fine."

"Just your gizzard. I know mine is in a wondrous twitch." Strix Strumajen's eyes began to leak tears again.

This is ridiculous, Lutta thought. She saw what Kreeth meant. Her own "gizzard" began to calm down a bit, and she was feeling slightly less nauseated.

"We sent so many out to look for you. Where were you, and how did you ever find us?" Grank asked.

"Oh, forgive me." Strix Strumajen turned to her daughter. "I have not even introduced you to our dear Grank. He is the chief counsel to King Hoole."

"Oh, yes, so pleased to meet you," Lutta said.

"He is regent in Hoole's absence," Strix Strumajen explained.

"Hoole isn't here?" Lutta tried to cover her surprise. If he wasn't in the great tree, it probably meant that the ember was not there, either. She had to be careful. "Where is he?"

"Out looking for you, my dear — and on other business as well," Strix Strumajen replied.

Better not appear too interested in this "other business." "I'm honored that a king should be looking for me." That must have been the appropriate answer because Strix Strumajen made a soft churring noise. "Don't be so modest, my dear. Your reputation as a close fighter and your courage in battle are well known." She sighed and thought, *If only my mate were alive and could see this magnificent daughter safe again.* There was indeed a stronger resemblance between her daughter and her dear mate, Hurthwel, than she had remembered. She shut her eyes briefly as if to stanch the memory and the sorrow.

Lutta had learned her lessons well. "Don't think of dear Da now, Mum. We are together."

"Yes, Emerilla, and it seems like a miracle. They said you had vanished over the Ice Fangs. What happened?"

Lutta was ready with her story. "It was almost like vanishing. Although there was no blood, I did suffer a terrible blow to my head and began to fall unconscious. And you're right, it was a miracle of sorts. I plummeted right onto the furry belly of a polar bear. Svin was his name, and I am forever grateful to him. He saved my life. Not only that — he tucked me away in his ice cave and tended me, bringing me fish. He even grabbed me a lemming once."

Curious, thought Grank. He had never heard of a polar bear going after a lemming, especially a polar bear of the Ice Fangs. And this region was not known for lemming communities.

"Believe me, Mum, I have had enough fish to last me a lifetime."

"Well, come with me, dear. We'll go to the dining hollow and you can have your fill of vole and some awfully good meadow mice."

After having supped, Strix Strumajen led her daughter to the hollow they would share. She had hoped that her daughter might be a bit more forthcoming as to how she had heard that her mother was here at the great tree and what she had been doing in these long moon cycles since she had been struck down in the Ice Fangs. Had her recovery taken all this time? But Emerilla was chary with her information and seemed more interested in the young king and the ember.

"You've heard about the ember, then?" Strix Strumajen asked.

"Oh yes, Mum. It's the talk of the Northern Kingdoms."

"But you were mostly with this polar bear, weren't you?"

"Yes, but Svin got out and about. He brought me news. But tell me, what is the young king like?"

"Oh, quite handsome. Very quick-witted. He's..." She paused. She had told Emerilla that Hoole was out looking for her, but she had not told her the other part of his mission, which was even more important: to set up a system of slipgizzles in the S'yrthghar. For some reason, she hesitated to tell Emerilla this. True, only the parliament knew the full extent of Hoole's mission. But why was she not eager to share everything with her daughter? She suddenly felt her gizzard give an alarming twinge. *What is happening? My gizzard should not be doing this.* She looked at her daughter again and marveled at how much she resembled her father.

Twice during that first day's sleep in the hollow, Strix Strumajen woke up and went over to where her daughter perched in a corner, sound asleep. Strix Strumajen peered at her, blinking, running her eyes over every little tuft, and gently preening her feathers as she had so longed to do. *Why am I not happier?* she thought. *Is there something wrong with me? I love her so much. Why do I have these strange feelings in my gizzard?* Finally, Strix Strumajen returned to her perch and fell into a deep sleep.

"Mum! Mum!" Emerilla was shaking her.

"What? What is it, dear? What time is it?"

"Nearly tween time. Can't you hear the cheering?"

"Yes! What is it?"

"The king has been spotted. He is approaching the tree."

"Oh, Great Glaux. He's back! How wonderful!"

"Yes, and won't he be surprised?"

"Why's that, dear?"

"Well, I'm here. The object of his search."

Strix Strumajen blinked. *How odd*, she thought, *and somewhat immodest*. Emerilla had always been so modest, so self-effacing.

"And the ember is back now, right? With him?"

"Why, it never left, dear," Strix Strumajen replied.

"Really?"

"Yes. It would be most cumbersome to carry around."

"But is it safe?"

"Why wouldn't it be safe?" She paused. "Emerilla, in this tree we have a bond of trust. Trust is really the essence of the Guardians of Ga'Hoole. You do understand that, don't you, darling? Trust was as much a part of our own family as the spots on our brows." She reached out and touched her daughter's brow that now so resembled the spiral of spots of her father's face. She felt Emerilla flinch slightly at her touch, and a dread began to seep into Strix Strumajen's gizzard. *Emerilla has changed in some way. That blow on her head has joggled something in her. Perhaps she needs a gizzard tonic. I shall consult with Grank.*

CHAPTER TWENTY-FOUR

An Assassination Attempt

In the Ice Palace of the H'rathghar glacier, a band of gadfeathers was making music, and a dozen owls led by Philma and Shadyk were dancing a flying quadrille. Servants were delivering piles of lemmings and a great quantity of bingle juice was being quaffed. Standing in the shadows, Theo watched with dismay as his brother roared drunken calls for the dancers.

> *Fly your partner round about,*
> *then spiral up and head on out.*
> *Flap your wings, then flutter on up.*
> *Here's a lemming for your sup.*

He staggered as he tried to land on the melting ice throne. To think that Hoole's father and grandfather, both such noble owls, had once sat there!

Sigrid, known only to Theo to be Emerilla, flew by with a lemming in each talon on her way to serve the guests. "Meet me at the northeast parapet when the moon's full up. News. We leave tonight," she whispered as she swept by Theo.

He had not planned to stay this long, but he needed more information to take back to the great tree. It was a race between how fast the Ice Palace was rotting and how fast other troops were approaching to lay siege. But now, finally, the end seemed to be in sight. Emerilla indeed was an owl of extraordinary intelligence and bravery. The risks she took every day, flying out under the cover of daylight to see what Lord Arrin's troops or the renegade packs of hagsfiends were up to, took enormous grit and daring. Yet here in the Ice Palace, she passed herself off as a most dutiful and diminished servant, enduring abuse from Shadyk and his bullying guards and councillors. The owls who served Shadyk as advisors were by no stretch of the imagination true councillors. They were only required to agree with him, to humor him and lavish praise upon him even when he was in a drunken stupor.

As the moon approached its highest point of the night, Theo began to fly through the winding corridors of ice that twisted up toward the four parapets. Shadows slid across the thin ice walls as owls danced jigs on the cold, rough night air to the music of a band of gadfeathers that were outside, singing on one of the parapets. Indeed, there appeared to be as much activity outside the ice palace as within. Theo even saw the shadow of a hagsfiend doing a palsied shuffle through the air, trying to keep time to the music.

Suddenly, however, shadows filled the corridor and blocked out the light of the moon and the stars. Theo's heart skipped a beat and his gizzard clenched. Two of Shadyk's largest guards were ahead. When he swiveled around, two more were coming up from behind. All four were armed with ice swords and scimitars. Theo had nothing — just his talons.

For an owl who hates fighting, he mused grimly, *I sure have to fight a lot.*

He scanned the narrow corridor to see if there was an icicle he could break off to use as a weapon but, with the ice rot, any such weapon would break immediately. The four owls were armed with ice weapons that either had been cut from healthy ice from the Ice Dagger or somewhere up in the Firth of Fangs. *Still,* thought Theo, *rotten ice might have its uses. I have to act fast.* He lofted himself straight up into the air. Theo was a powerful owl with powerful wings. The ceiling of the corridor was low, and the owls were surprised that he would try to fly above them. They raised their ice scimitars, but Theo was a cunning flyer as well as fast. He extended his wings as widely as he could and sheered off the stanchions of rotting ice, which then fell in heaps on the corridor floor. Next, there was a great creaking as the ceiling began to collapse behind him. The owls' way was blocked. Suddenly, he saw Emerilla flying toward him. He heard a clatter behind him and turned. One of the smaller guards had managed to fly over the heap of collapsed ice. The corridor had narrowed drastically, and Theo did not have room to turn.

"Against the wall! Let me pass!" Emerilla shouted to him. He pressed himself against the melting ice wall and gaped as Emerilla charged the guard who had his cutlass raised. There was a small spurt of blood and then disbelief in the guard's eyes as he looked down and saw his guts hanging out of his belly.

So this is close fighting! Theo silently exclaimed.

Now three other guards were scrambling over the pile of ice shards. Emerilla had picked up the cutlass of the fallen guard and tossed it to Theo. Together, the Great Horned and the Spotted Owl advanced on the three remaining assassins. It was as if Theo's and Emerilla's minds had become one. Theo knew that his task was to keep the three other owls engaged by quick parrying with his cutlass. For all intents and purposes, Emerilla, the stupid serving lass, did not appear to have a weapon. The three guards, to their mortal detriment, hardly paid her any heed. When the second owl collapsed — minus half of his port wing — the two others looked down in shock. "Kill her!" One screamed. "Shadyk will have our heads."

"No!" Theo roared and, picking up the rapier of the fallen owl, powered straight up, a weapon in each talon, stabbing one guard in the gizzard and the other in the heart. The corridor was slick with blood.

Then there was a huge clapping sound like thunder. "The northeast parapet! It's falling!" Emerilla cried out. And from a hole in the wall, they saw it tumbling through the night. "Follow me," Emerilla shouted.

They flew out through a hole in the corridor wall and headed south toward Stormfast Island. As Theo looked back, havoc reigned in the Ice Palace. Hagsfiends were taking flight as the entire eastern side of the palace caved in. An icy wind came up announcing the first of the serious winter storms driven by the N'yrthnookah, the northeast wind that brought the heaviest of the blizzards. With this wind behind them, they made a short business of the flight to Stormfast. The dawn was just breaking when they arrived.

"There's a good ice hollow on the lee side of the island. We'll get protection from all this," Emerilla said.

Once in the hollow, Emerilla looked up at Theo. "So, before you were so rudely interrupted by the guards on your way to see me, I had been planning to tell you the latest news."

"Yes, but how did you know to come down that corridor and not wait for me on the parapet?"

"Just a feeling in the gizzard. I just suddenly sensed that Shadyk was going to do something tonight."

"You fought brilliantly."

"Well, you weren't so bad yourself."

"So what is the news?"

"Lord Arrin is massing a huge force."

"But I thought his followers had left him."

"They had, but one important one has returned: Lord Elgobad."

"Lord Elgobad?"

"Yes, do you know him?"

"In a sense. A Snowy. He attacked me some time ago in the Bitter Sea. I wounded him, but I guess not mortally."

"Well, he has joined forces with Lord Arrin once again. They plan to lay siege to the Ice Palace."

"There won't be much left of it."

"This N'yrthnookah will delay the ice rot."

"I guess that's both good news and bad news," Theo said.

"Yes, it buys time for King Hoole," Emerilla replied. "Is he ready to fight?"

"I hope so. He had gone on a long mission into the S'yrthghar. He wanted to get colliers and blacksmiths."

"Ah, yes, for the new weapons. I have heard about them. Battle claws they call them."

Theo closed his eyes and nodded his head sadly.

"What's wrong, Theo?" Emerilla asked.

"I am the one who made those first battle claws."

"But why does that make you so sad?"

"It is, my dear" — he felt he could call her "my dear" as he was so much older than she — "a sad thing to have as a legacy the creation of a new and deadly weapon."

"I see," Emerilla said softly.

CHAPTER TWENTY-FIVE

"Who Am I? What Am I?"

"That's it! That's it, Emerilla! You would think she had been hatched with battle claws! Just look at her parry with them," Grank exclaimed with delight to Strix Strumajen.

"Well, she's known for being excellent with the close blade and has remarkable turning ability," Strix Strumajen said proudly.

"But her flight balance is perfect and a close blade is so much smaller and lighter than these battle claws," Phineas said.

Grank! Phineas! Lutta wondered. *Even that old codger Lord Rathnik comments on my skill, but why doesn't Hoole notice me?*

"Mum," she said, "Hoole never seems to see my best parries and rebounds."

Strix Strumajen chuckled. "He sees you, my dear, but he has much on his mind. He must supervise the training of all these owls and the new recruits."

Hoole had been back for less than a moon cycle and, within that time, Lutta was captivated by this strong, handsome young owl. It was a strange and wonderful feeling. Strix Strumajen's initial gizzardly reservations about her daughter had quietly disappeared. Indeed, her daughter seemed much more like her old self. *Ah, what a first infatuation can do!* Strix Strumajen thought. Of course, who knew if Hoole felt anything for Emerilla? She was certainly attractive enough in every way, but poor Hoole had so many worries. It was not exactly the right time in his life for romance. Although he did seem quite impressed with Emerilla and often invited both her and her mother for milkberry tea in his hollow, it was usually to discuss war strategy.

Excellent progress had been made at the great tree. Rupert the Rogue smith from Ambala and two other colliers had accompanied Hoole back from the S'yrthghar. Phineas and the Snow Rose had rounded up three other Rogue smiths and two more colliers. It would have been best if Theo had been present to instruct the smiths in the art of forging battle claws, but Grank had learned quite a bit from observing Theo and was a very good instructor. And, of course, no owl could equal Grank in colliering. At this point, there were robust fires going in a half-dozen forges near the tree. The fires were so productive in terms of battle claws that there seemed to be little energy left in the flames to reveal anything of great significance to either Hoole or Grank as to what was occurring in the N'yrthghar. But as soon as any message came from Theo, they would be off. Joss had flown out a few nights before to try to make contact with Theo and come back with a report.

Other members of the parliament had been dispatched to muster troops from the Shadow Forest — Tyto, Ambala, and Silverveil. Each day, new owls arrived and were being trained. When the call came, they would be ready.

Lutta, looking like Emerilla to the feather, had taken a break from her practice and went to observe Hoole as he worked with a young Barn Owl. She watched him as he tied on the battle claws.

"When you wear these, it's important to fly with your talons lifted up just a bit. It helps counterbalance the weight of the claws." He gave the young owl a friendly cuff. Emerilla felt something shimmer deep within her. This was not the first time she had experienced this sensation. But she was unsure what exactly she was feeling. It happened several times a day. She told herself it was nothing to do with a gizzard. *I don't have a gizzard. This is impossible. I cannot have any gizzardly feelings. Nothing will get in my way,* she told herself as she continued to watch.

"Now, Winfyr," Hoole said, addressing the young owl, "after you get used to flying with these battle claws, we'll let you try winging around with the close blade." He paused and swiveled his head toward Lutta. "There's your expert on the close blade, right there." He nodded at her and Lutta thought she might fall from her perch. Then suddenly, she had an idea. A perfect excuse for meeting with Hoole, possibly alone in his hollow!

"Now, what is this idea of yours, Emerilla?" Hoole said, settling on a perch. She was so excited to finally be alone in his company that she hardly knew how to start. She perched in front of the iron teardrop-shaped container of the ember. The ember's glow seemed to fill the hollow. Every time she had seen it, it never failed to stir her. It reminded her of her task, of the power that she and Kreeth would have.

And if, she thought, *if I can make him mine forever . . .* She felt a terrible cramp inside her and the ember emitted a low hiss and cast a glowing light. *Would he come to me on his own? And would he come to me if he knew who I really was?*

Lutta engaged in endless dialogues like this whenever she was in the presence of the ember. Inner monologues that led to no conclusion, except she was left with a confused, unfinished feeling and often a question. *Who am I? What am I?*

Finally, she pushed these thoughts from her mind. "Your Majesty, when I was watching you train the young Barn Owl, it came to me that perhaps I might be helpful teaching them to fight with the close blade. I thought maybe I could help my mother with her classes."

Hoole's eyes blinked open and shut several times. "What an excellent idea. I should have thought of it myself. Why, with both you and Strix teaching, we could train an entire squadron of close-bladers. You could be the co-commander."

"Really?!"

"Yes, really. This could prove indispensable. We have many who can fight with the larger ice weapons — scimitars, pikes, swords — and then there are the very smallest of owls — like Phineas — who are terrific with the ice splinters. But how many really good close-blade owls do we have? With a squadron of close-bladers, we'll have much more range, much more flexibility in every combat situation." He paused and looked at Lutta with what she felt was a new light in his eyes. "You're quite clever, Emerilla."

"Clever, sir?"

At that moment, there was a rap on the edge of the

hollow. A young Snowy poked his head in. "Coded message, sir. Grank is on his way."

"Oh, good. Good!" Hoole turned to Lutta. "Well, thank you so much. You must excuse me now."

Lutta remained on the perch. Hoole stared at her. "I said, you must excuse me."

"Oh, I do." But she remained on the perch.

Hoole cocked his head. "Do you understand what I am saying, Emerilla? It means you have to leave."

Grank had just arrived and was observing this peculiar exchange.

"Oh!" She lofted herself off the perch and flew by Grank, almost knocking him over.

"Strange one, she is," Grank murmured.

"A bit odd. But what is this message?"

"Well," Grank said, swiveling his head to make sure that both Emerilla and the young Snowy were gone, "let's go in there to read it." He nodded toward a perch that protruded from a crack.

To the ordinary owl's eyes, the crack in the wall of the hollow looked like any other crack in the interior of a tree. A perch had been jammed into it. But when Hoole reached up with his talons and yanked the perch, out came a piece of a milkberry vine. With one pull, a panel opened and, through it, the two owls crowded into a smaller space. They shut the panel behind them. It was a secret chamber in the tree that Hoole and Grank had worked on for several days and in which they read the coded messages sent by Joss.

Grank unfurled the piece of birch bark that the message was inscribed on and began to read. "'The ice worms turn. The lice do swarm. A burning teardrop will set it to rights.'"

Grank looked at Hoole. "And so the Ice Palace is rotting."

"'Lord Arrin and Elgobad unite and make ready to attack.' But Grank, is this right? Must I bring the ember? Is that truly what the message means?"

"To stop the rot, the ember's power is needed."

"But it is foolhardy to travel with it."

"Yes." Grank blinked. "Let me give some thought to this before we leave."

"Good, but first the parliament must meet. We must work out a detailed invasion strategy."

"The usual passage into the N'yrthghar is through the Ice Narrows." Hoole was pointing with his talon to a map, which had been etched out on a dried rabbit hide with a stick of charred wood, as he spoke to the members of the parliament. "But now that we number in the hundreds, it seems unwise that our entire force should try to squeeze through this narrow passage and become vulnerable to ambush. Instead, let us try the unexpected." There was a low mumbling of assent among the ten other members of the parliament.

"Surprise can be as deadly as any weapon," Lord Rathnik said.

"Indeed! Indeed!" echoed several owls.

"My plan is this," Hoole continued. "Even though the Ice Narrows is the shortest and the most direct route, with the N'yrthnookah blowing we would be flying dead into the wind and arrive pretty ragged and exhausted. If we flew off the wind a bit, taking a long way around, we would conserve our energy and also have a better chance of escaping detection."

"A question here, Your Grace." A Northern Hawk owl, Sir Tobyfyor, raised a talon.

"Yes, Sir Toby?"

"I presume you are talking about going by way of Broken Talon Point, but hundreds of owls flying over Broken Talon Point will not go unnoticed."

"We will go by three routes: Broken Talon Point, as well as the point off the spirit woods, and due east to the far shore of the S'yrthghar sea. I know that eastern route is a rarely used one, but once over that shore we could claw north on a close-wing reach and fly around the end of the Ice Narrows. If Sir Bors and his students in the navigational chaw would provide us with the star maps, it would be most useful. These routes have rarely been flown."

"Aaah." A sound of approval rolled through the parliament.

"Strix Strumajen, can you give us any insight into atmospheric pressure changes that we should be expecting?"

"It's a little far in the future for accurate predictions. But there is a series of smee holes just inland from that eastern shore. They are quite active this time of year and should provide a robust thermal boost that could give us a nice bounce right over the N'yrthnookah. Indeed, I would suggest dispatching at least two regiments in that direction. There is ample territory for them to spread out so they won't draw a lot of attention. And the eastern shore region is little inhabited, save for some eagles."

"Brilliant, Strix Strumajen!" Grank exclaimed.

Perhaps, she thought to herself. *But I wish Emerilla could help me here. She used to be so sensitive to any atmospheric pressure variation. It must be that blow on the head!*

So an invasion strategy was devised. There would be three contingents, the smallest of which would be a squad of eight or nine owls to fly through the Ice Narrows, hopefully not drawing too much attention. They would depart in relays, leaving time in between each group. Then several platoons would fly to Cape Glaux and turn north, threading their way through the spirit woods to meet up with platoons that had flown over Broken Talon Point. Together, they would form a regiment. Finally, an entire division would fly due east from the island to the eastern shore and then turn north. They would hold these formations for the attack in the H'rathghar. Whether Lord Arrin would be holding the palace was unknown. The battle might in fact occur in the ridge lands of the H'rathghar glacier. The location of old stashes of ice weapons — for they were not depending entirely on battle claws — had also been discussed. The first squads, those bound for Broken Talon and Cape Glaux, would leave at daybreak. Shortly after, the rest would depart.

Later that evening, Hoole told Lutta that he had assigned her to fly in what was now being called the Eastern Regiment.

"But that isn't really the right assignment for me, Hoole," she protested.

"No?" He blinked at her. They were alone in his hollow once again.

"When I came here, I flew through the Ice Narrows. The wind was blowing fiercely from the south for several days before I arrived. I was forced to take refuge in an ice hollow with a family of puffins — not the brightest, mind you — but they showed me something fascinating."

"What was that?"

"A huge weapons stash."

"Really?"

"Yes — close blades." She paused. "I should take the squadron I have been training. We'll collect the extra blades. We don't have enough right now as it is. I can handle two blades at once. One in each talon." She blinked, then narrowed her eyes. Two glowering slits. The glow of the ember cast her face in an odd light. Hoole's gizzard gave a lurch.

"Let me go there, Hoole. With two close blades and a set of battle claws, I'll fight like you've never seen an owl fight."

Hoole looked at her oddly. There *was* something strange about this owl. Her intensity almost unnerved him, yet she was fascinating. She stirred in him something vaguely familiar. A confusion of feelings. It suddenly dawned on Hoole. *She's not unlike the ember.*

"Are you all right, Your Majesty? Is something wrong?" Lutta asked.

"No, no, I'm fine. And you say there are enough weapons for the rest in your squad?"

"Yes, of course . . . and Hoole . . ."

"Yes, Emerilla?"

Her gaze had softened and she seemed to be looking far off, almost as if she was in a trance.

"Emerilla, what is it? Did you have something more you wanted to say?"

Lutta shook her head rapidly, almost violently. "Oh nothing, Your Majesty, nothing at all." But of course she had so much more to say. The words pressed against her beak. She wanted to say, "And when this is over, we'll be together, forever, always. I'll be your queen." No, just his mate — that would be enough. She began to feel a deep ache within her. "Just his mate." These three words surprised Lutta as much as anything. They were true. She did not care about being a queen. She just wanted to belong, that was all. A dread crept through her. *This cannot be. I don't have a gizzard! I don't have a gizzard!*

CHAPTER TWENTY-SIX
Not the Ember!

"What? What do you mean it's not the ember?"

"It's a fraud, you idiot."

Kreeth swatted Lutta with a broad wing across her now darkly feathered face. Lutta had shed the plumage of a Spotted Owl. It had been a brilliant transformation. She had been leading her squad of owls through the Narrows according to Hoole's battle plan, then had flown ahead around a bend. Mere seconds later, she flew out again, no longer a Spotted Owl but a full-blown hagsfiend. The shock of the owls in the squad had thrilled her. Three had actually gone yeep before she could even cast a fyngrot. The four others attempted to fight, but Lutta had come back with an ice scimitar and made quick work of them. She did not waste any time collecting their heads, but flew back immediately to the deserted great tree and seized the ember.

But now Kreeth was telling her that this was not the ember.

"But it looks exactly like the one in Hoole's hollow. And look at this tear-shaped box it is in."

"I will claw your eyes out!" Kreeth flew at Lutta who wrapped her wings around her face.

"No! No! Don't!"

"Then get it for me, you fool."

"He must have substituted this ember for the real one. He ... he ... he didn't trust me." And at that moment something broke in Lutta. A gizzard?

From the air, the ridge lands of the H'rathghar glacier were a series of sawtooth ice crests that swelled in waves for nearly as far as the eye could see. It was at the edge of these ridge lands that the Ice Palace rose, now half its former size. With no hagsfiends to guard it, and an insane imposter king inside with only a handful of troops, the palace was defenseless. Yet taking it would be far from easy. Not with Lord Arrin's troops amassing on the other side of it. Even from where Hoole perched, he could see the darker-than-night ragged shadows draped on those far ridges. Lord Arrin had reconstituted his hagsfiend regiment and combined them with those of Elgobad and every other renegade and outlaw. All these enemies of the old regime, with its codes of honor and nobility, were now gathered to take the palace.

Around Hoole's neck the ember hung in a battered

vial, much like the ones Frost Beak masters wore to carry their ice-splinter repair kits.

"I can't understand where the Ice Narrows squad is," Hoole wondered aloud. "They should have been here by now." Hoole looked at his troops. They were a motley army. The guardians of the parliament as befitted their stations looked quite formidable with their battle claws, ice sabers, cutlasses, and scimitars. Then there were the hireclaws from the S'yrthghar as well as others who had come because of their love of Hoole. Many more came to fight in honor of Hoole's mother, the late Queen Siv. Large numbers of them had followed Siv into the Battle of the Beyond. They called themselves the Sivian Guard. Predominantly female, they were incredibly fierce and very skilled with both battle claws and ice scimitars. They were commanded by Strix Strumajen whom they adored.

Hoole glanced now toward Strix Strumajen, erect on her perch, scanning the horizon for her daughter. He knew she was a stalwart soldier and would not let Emerilla's second disappearance distract her from the task at hand. But then Hoole blinked. He saw something moving through the darkness, low to the ground. He blinked again. What were those slivers of green, like rips in the black of the night?

"Great Glaux," he whispered to himself, "it's Namara."

He had left her in Ambala and she had made her way back to her den in the region of Broken Talon Point. But here she was, coming with legions of wolves: more, many more than had gone with her into the Desert of Kuneer. They were settling in at the base of the ridge, but Namara herself was advancing up the steep grade toward Hoole.

"Namara!"

"Yes, Commander." She crouched down and laid her ears back flat and then scraped forward on her belly in the attitude of complete submission practiced by wolves when approaching a superior.

"Get up!" Hoole intensely disliked the elaborate formalities of rank that governed the lives of wolves.

"But you are my commander."

"I might command an army, but you, Namara, will always be my equal. What are you here for?"

"To fight, sir. We are the Sky Dogs of the Beyond. And look carefully, sir, and you will see something else amongst us."

Hoole blinked, then squinted his eyes and blinked again. There was a slight quivering movement within the huge pack of wolves. "Pygmies, Elves, Northern Saw-whets!" All of the tiniest owls in the owl kingdoms, all veterans of the Frost Beak divisions that had scattered after being driven from the N'yrthghar during the long war. They were close fighters and their weapons of choice were deadly ice splinters. Hoole shook his head in dismay. It was brilliant, absolutely brilliant. There was nothing that could compare to the strategic thinking of a wolf, and now Namara had had the inspired idea of combining small owls with wolves into an elite fighting force.

"When are you planning to attack?" Namara asked.

"We were waiting for a squad that seems to have vanished somewhere in the Ice Narrows."

"And if they come soon?"

"Then we'll attack."

"May I offer a suggestion, Hoole?"

"Of course, Namara."

"You are ideally situated on this ridge. You are facing west. The enemy is facing east. Wait until daybreak."

"Daybreak?" Daybreak was a long way off.

"Wait until the sun is nearly the length of a high leaping wolf."

"Why?" And then it dawned on Hoole. Of course! If they attacked at daybreak, the enemy would be blinded by the rising sun. More than blinded, for shards of light as sharp as a sword's edge would bounce off the ice-sheathed ridges of the glacier.

Hoole called together his lieutenants and the members of the parliament. He paused before he spoke. *Oh*

Glaux, he thought, *steel my soldiers' hearts. Make trim their gizzards for this fight. Give me the words that will burn like the Rogue smiths' metal and pierce with the keenness of a blade cut from the heart of the Ice Dagger. Protect these noble owls. How I envy the ease of their gizzards and do wish that sometimes I were not born a prince, or had to be a king.*

Then he explained the strategy and told them of Namara and the Sky Dog Unit.

There was so much to be done, and Hoole knew that even if they won by the blessings of all that was Glaux, and though he planned to rule from the great tree, the task of clearing the rot from his father's palace, restoring the throne and the kingdom to what it had been in the days of the H'rathian code was a monumental task. But he did not mean to get ahead in his thoughts. First, a most decisive battle must be won. So he put his private thoughts away and began to address his troops.

"Dear owls, it troubles me not if another might wear my crown, or sit upon a throne that now rots inside a melting palace. That is only the outer show, and I do not care for such outward things as they do not make the owl. But I do yearn for honor, and for honor I shall be the most ferocious owl alive. This night to come is called the Long Night. He and she who live out this day and night to see old age will yearly, in celebration of it, fly high, tip their wings, show their scars, and say, 'These wounds I did suffer in the Battle of the Short Light and the Long Night.' Old owls shall remember what feats they did that day. And our names will be spoken in hollows and become familiar to all — Strix Strumajen, Rathnik, Garthnore, Bors, and Tobyfyor. Each good owl will tell their sons and daughters of this, the Battle of the Short Light and the Long Night and, in the telling, you shall be remembered from this day to the ending of the world.

"So once more into the breach, dear friends, to halt that rotting from within, or close the gaps in those sickly walls with our dead. I say to you that in peace there is nothing that becomes an owl as much as a quiet stillness and humility, but when the roar of war blasts in our ears, let us stiffen our wings and fly with a hardened rage."

CHAPTER TWENTY-SEVEN
Into the Short Light

And so they waited for the Short Light. Waited through the thick darkness of the night and then the thinning of the black into deep gray. They watched as that gray dissolved, becoming a pale transparence before the dawn. Hoole swiveled his head toward the east and watched as a blush crept over the horizon. The pink reddened and the sky became hectic with color as the sun began to rise. He could feel the tension of his army. He counted quietly to himself and at precisely one hundred twenty-two seconds after the sun was over the horizon, Namara leaped high into the air. The sun flared off her silver coat. This was the signal.

"Hi-yaaaa!" Hoole roared. First off the ridge were the Hot Claws of Hoole, commanded by the king himself, then the Sivian Guard led by Strix Strumajen. Next came the Ice Regiment of H'rath, captained by Lord Rathnik. The other squads, platoons, and regiments followed. All flew low so as not to block the fiery blades of the sun from the enemies' eyes. A ranger owl slid in next to Hoole. "Your Majesty, Theo and a small squadron have been spotted coming from the south."

Hoole was tempted to look south, but he could not let himself be distracted. He and his forces had the advantage now. He could see the enemy troops in chaos. Even the hagsfiends were having trouble mustering a fyngrot in the growing brightness of the Short Light. Hoole knew that he and his troops must not squander the advantage bestowed by the sunrise. The enemy would fly out and then, blasted by the glare, come to ground where the Sky Dogs — the wolves and the tiny owls of the Frost Beaks — would attack. While training the troops on the island, Hoole tried to adapt some of the strategies that the wolves practiced for his owl armies, in particular, the subtle signaling system used by the wolves in their byrrgis formations. Hoole cocked his tail feathers and that signal swept through the Hoolian troops. The army split into four divisions and took command of four strategic ridges, two of which had been occupied by the enemy. On these four ridges, Hoole's troops would rest and reinforce. Scouts were sent out to count the dead and collect discarded ice weapons. The report was promising. The hagsfiends' fyngrot had been useless in the glare of the Short Light, and now scores of hagsfiends lay dead. Lord Arrin's troops had been pushed back farther than Hoole had dared hope for, but they were still a threat, not yet near full retreat. In the Long Night to come, Hoole knew that the battle would rage on. Hoole touched the vial with the ember. He could feel its glow. *Magic will not win a battle,* he thought. But magic might restore the Ice Palace of his forebears, the once magnificent structure that appeared to be in watery shambles. What had taken a thousand N'yrthghar winters to build, from warping winds, raging blizzards, and ice storms, had collapsed within a few short cycles of the moon. Hoole blinked as he saw a lone owl in a jagged flight over the last standing turret. "Who is that mad owl?" Hoole spoke to himself.

"My brother, sir," Theo said.

"Theo!" Hoole was stunned. "Theo, you are here!"

"Yes, my squadron is on that next ridge." He indicated with a twitch of his head.

"And that owl you say is your brother?" Hoole did not even know that Theo had a brother.

"Yes, he took over the Ice Palace with a ragtag army of idiots and hagsfiends. He is completely mad. He tried to kill me. He is the cause of the rotting ice."

Hoole touched the vial and felt once more its heat.

"By the way," Theo began, obviously wanting to change the subject, "your lessons from the wolves are good ones."

"I'm glad."

"We are using the byrrgis formation and the wolves' signaling system. Oh, I nearly forgot. I have found Emerilla. I must tell Strix Strumajen. She saved my life, you know."

"What?" Hoole was thoroughly confused. "You found Emerilla? *She saved your life?* When?"

"Yes, when my brother tried to assassinate me."

"But that is impossible!"

At that precise moment, there was a cry from Lord Rathmik. "They're coming! They're coming!" And the last drop of light slid beneath the horizon to another morning somewhere far away. The Short Light was finished.

"Great Glaux!" Hoole blinked wildly. He had never seen anything like this. A hundred hagsfiends followed by hundreds of owls. Hoole had never expected them to recover so quickly, and where had these additional troops come from? *Oh, the Long Night has come!* thought Hoole. *And we must fly out to meet it!*

CHAPTER TWENTY-EIGHT

Into the Long Night

The night was torn with blood and the flash of ice swords and battle claws in the moonlight. In his starboard metal-clawed talon, Hoole carried the ice scimitar of his father, the very same one his mother had used in the Battle of the Beyond. More than the ember, it was this ice scimitar that emboldened him. And just as the scimitar had infused Siv with a concentration that seemed to resist the paralyzing effect of the deadly yellow light, so now did it sustain Hoole. But it was not the scimitar alone that inspired him. It was the memories of his mother's valor. He felt the gallgrot rise within him as he slashed through the fyngrot, cutting a swath for his troops to follow. *What cowards those traitorous owls are to hide behind the yellow glare,* he thought.

"Fight like an owl of honor!" Hoole cried out. Elgobad and Arrin with their flanking captains, Snowy, and an immense Great Gray, melted from behind the last remnants of the glare. Strix Strumajen and Theo rushed in behind Hoole. The three advanced upon the two lords and their captains. Three against four. The four enemy owls all fought with long swords so it was difficult to get close with only battle claws. The ice weapons that Theo, Hoole, and Strix Strumajen carried were shorter than the long swords of the enemy, but they were also sharper. Hoole had anticipated this when training the owls on the island. He silently gave the signal for the parry-and-feint maneuver. All three began a forward skipping motion with an abrupt swerve, and then a violent backstroking of the wings. The long swords of the enemy pointed here, then there, trying to keep up with this odd aerial jig. This maneuver was used to open a clear space for attack with short weapons. Once, twice, three more times, a very small space opened. *Too small!* cursed Hoole, but suddenly there was a spray of blood. Lord Elgobad plummeted. From the corner of his eye, he saw a young Spotted Owl peel off to port.

"Emerilla!" The name exploded in the night, and in that moment Strix Strumajen realized that here was the real Emerilla, and the creature who had called herself her daughter was guilty of a most heinous deception.

That false creature now perched on an icy peak with her creator and regarded the battle that raged. Kreeth narrowed her eyes and saw the bouncing movements of the vial that Hoole wore around his neck. "There is your ember,

Lutta." As the old hag watched, she saw isolated patches of fyngrot scattered through the battlefield. The owls of Lord Arrin were now exposed. More fyngrot was needed, and although Kreeth herself did not care which side won or lost this stupid war — for all she wanted was the power of the ember — she now saw that it would be to her advantage to reinforce the existing fyngrots with her own. She knew that her own fyngrot had an intense potency because she had not recklessly squandered it in silly wars. This, however, would not be reckless, nor would it be squandered. She had one goal in mind: to seize the ember. *Then leave them to fight over that rotting palace,* she thought.

Lutta herself had remained in her hagsfiend form. Kreeth had to admit that Lutta was a beautiful fiend. The blackness of her feathers had a hint of deep blue and her plumage poured off her body like dark glistening flames. But now it was time for the transformation back into a Spotted Owl, a close fighter, as was her true counterpart, Emerilla.

Lutta shut her eyes tightly and began to concentrate. In her mind's eye, she saw the spots that spiraled out like small galaxies from the center of the top of her head. She swore she felt the streaks of white begin to break up the dark plumage of her breast.

"What's wrong with you?" Kreeth muttered.

Lutta blinked and looked down at her breast feathers. There were white spots and streaks but the rest of the feathers were still blue-black. She peered into Kreeth's eyes and gasped at the reflection she saw in them. There were smears of white on her head, but again the feathers were not the tawny browns and ambers of a Spotted Owl. She was, in fact, half hagsfiend and half Spotted Owl. The owl part of her winced now at her own malodorous breath.

"You're not doing it!" Kreeth cursed and dark spittle ran from her beak.

"I know! I know! I don't know why — I don't understand."

But in truth, Lutta did understand. She was sick; sick of being half: half crow, half owl, both hagsfiend and Spotted Owl. She was, she realized, nothing. She was nothing and yet she loved. "I have a gizzard!" she screamed at her creator.

"You do not have a gizzard, you fool, you idiot. I created you."

"You created me, but I created this gizzard."

Kreeth was stunned. "No!" she exploded and gave Lutta a thwack that nearly sent her tumbling from the peak. Lutta rose up in pain and hovered above Kreeth. "You don't understand, Kreeth! I feel pain. Real pain."

"It's a phantom gizzard."

"What difference does it make, be it phantom or real? I love him. I love him."

"You must kill him," Kreeth hissed. Then a narrow beam of yellow light sprung from her eyes. Lutta felt herself go yeep.

"Down you go, dearie. Down, down, down. Right here by my talons. Nice soft landing."

On a distant ridge, the eyes of a large Great Horned Owl and his hagsfiend consort were fixed on the scene that was transpiring.

"She used the fyngrot on Lutta. I can't believe it!" Ygyrk gasped. "It's wrong. Wrong to use it on one" — she hesitated and then said the next words with great vehemence — "one of your own."

Pleek blinked at her in surprise, which for some reason irritated Ygryk. "Yes, Pleek, she is ours," she hissed. "Even monsters can have some honor."

"You're not a monster, my dear," Pleek replied. Ygryk's hard black eyes bore into him. She knew exactly what was going through his mind, which he was too afraid to say: *You are not a monster. Lutta is. She's a freak.*

"No, Pleek."

"No what?"

"The problem is not with Lutta. The problem is with us."

"What are you talking about?"

"She is not the freak. We are." She paused. "We don't know how to love."

When Lutta woke up, she looked down and saw the tawny brown feathers of a Spotted Owl. *So she's done it. Made me Emerilla again. Cast a spell, I suppose. But what am I really?*

She watched as Kreeth rose in the night; beneath the moon a yellow glare began to spread. The H'rathian Guard felt their wings still, then the Sivian guard wavered in flight. Hundreds of troops were brought to ground — to ground for slaughter. Hoole suddenly sensed the quietness on the glacial battlefield. He turned and flinched. This indeed was a powerful fyngrot. He rose, holding high the scimitar of his father, King H'rath, of his mother, Queen Siv. He knew that he must fly directly into the yellow glare. He had done it before. He would do it again. The hagsfiend who hovered as she cast her light was immense and old and ragged. He saw her wing feathers stirring with half-hags, and then he thought he saw a Spotted Owl flying close to her, but he was not sure. Hoole's gizzard clenched as he saw the noble Lord Rathnik fall in flight and a swarm of half-hags fly from the hagsfiend's plummels to nibble on the falling lord. He was dead by the time he hit the ground.

Not one more owl of honor must die, Hoole thought. He raised the scimitar and charged the light. He cut through it, but weakly. *Glaux, this is a tough fyngrot,* Hoole thought.

Suddenly, there were slits of green in the night. The wolves! Hundreds of wolves raced to the top of the ridge and though not commanded, the green of their eyes began to crisscross the fyngrot, weaving through the warp of the yellow glare like a shuttle with threads of green. *It's breaking up! It's breaking up!* Hoole silently rejoiced. At last, the fyngrot ripped. And the black trail of the Long Night ran through it. All over, feathers began to rustle and stir — spotted, tawny, pure white. Primary feathers began to stiffen, and owls who had been brought to ground spread their wings to rise, and those who had begun to go yeep regained altitude. The fyngrot was no more.

Then out of the unsullied darkness a Spotted Owl flew.

"Emerilla!" Hoole gasped.

A shriek tore through the night. "The ember, Lutta! Get the ember, or I shall curse you forever!"

A wolf, one Duncan MacDuncan, leaped high into the sky where a gnarled and screeching hagsfiend and her half-hags had begun to go yeep in the fierce blades of the green light. The lone wolf yanked her to the ground, ripped out her eyes, which were pulsing a dim yellow, and sank his fangs into the hagsfiend's neck.

A huge cheer rose from the armies of Hoole. "To the Ice Palace!" Hundreds of owls surged over the last ridges, followed by still more wolves. Then Hoole caught sight of Theo's battle claws shining under the moon, summoning him. "King Hoole!"

Hoole forgot Emerilla and in a quick flip reversed his direction and flew toward the crumbling palace, leading the divisions of his armies; below the wolves clambered up the ice-sheathed ramparts.

CHAPTER TWENTY-NINE

The Ice Palace

"Emerilla?" Hoole blinked at the owl who perched beside Theo in the dripping walls of the throne room. This owl looked like Emerilla but even more so. How could that be?

"You know me?" the Spotted Owl asked. She was confused. Why was this owl, the king, studying her so?

"Of course I know you," his voice was soft and intimate. "I was concerned that something had happened to you when you came through the Ice Narrows."

"Ice Narrows?" Emerilla was confounded. "I was never in the Ice Narrows."

"But I did fly through the Ice Narrows." The voice came from behind him. A silence fell on the crowd of owls and wolves. Only the drip...drip...drip of the rotting ice could be heard. Another Spotted Owl stood in a puddle of melted ice.

"Emerilla?" Hoole turned around and saw an owl almost identical to the one he had just spoken to. She looked exactly like Emerilla. No . . . no . . . not quite exactly. The tips of her tawny wings were beginning to turn black. Lutta was changing before his very eyes. The owl he thought he knew as Emerilla was dissolving into a dark crowlike thing that was now flying directly toward him. He felt himself suddenly skid across the ice and slam into the melting throne. His eyes closed momentarily, and when he opened them, he saw Strix Strumajen hovering over a strange heap of black and brown feathers. The puddle of water was turning red with blood. Little gnat-like creatures floated dead on its surface.

"Half-hags!" the two words swept through the throne room.

"I had to kill her," Strix Strumajen said. "She pretended to be my Emerilla. I knew from the start that something was not right about her. A blood deception she was — a hagsfiend."

"No!" a whispery voice rose from the pile of feathers. Hoole flew over to her.

"What are you?" he asked, peering down at the dying creature.

"I am nothing, and yet I loved . . ."

The vial of the ember dangled from Hoole's neck. She lifted a talon.

She wants the ember! Hoole thought.

"No, it is not the ember I wanted." Lutta whispered, and died.

From the pile of feathers a foggy shape rose, like a shadow made of mist. It rose and then dissolved as the spirit of Lutta passed away.

"To hagsmire," muttered Strix Strumajen. She turned to the real Emerilla. "Oh, daughter," she sighed and folded her into her wings.

Hoole gazed at Emerilla. Her spots shimmered like a galaxy of stars. It was as if glaumora had come down to earth.

At last, thought Hoole. And his own gizzard quaked with something warm and genuine and new.

There was a sudden quietness in the throne hollow. "Nothing is dripping," Theo whispered with excitement.

"The melting has stopped," Phineas said.

"Look at the throne!" The Snow Rose lofted herself into the air and flew over the ice throne.

"To the throne, Your Majesty. To the throne!"

So Hoole took his rightful place, and the moment he perched on the throne of that noble family of the N'yrthghar, the throne stopped melting and began to glow with new ice. Hoole felt the warmth of the ember against his chest. And he knew that although the ember's magic could not win a war it could restore a kingdom with a righteous ruler. This was the lesson of the ember. He flew to the highest ice spindle on the throne. He held the vial with the ember that now glowed an iridescent, mysterious green. "Just as the stars do not hold our destinies, this ember holds not our fate. We are masters of our own fate, dear friends. The days to come will be ones of hope and glory." A great cheer rose up. *Yes, hope and glory,* thought Hoole. *And perhaps love, as well.*

And indeed the days and the years that followed were ones of hope and glory and love. Emerilla and Hoole found happiness together as mates. They had owlets, one of whom, H'rathruyan, became the regent of the Ice Palace of the N'yrthghar. But no one called it the N'yrthghar any longer. It became known as the Northern Kingdoms as the S'yrthghar was known only as the Southern Kingdoms. And the southern sea became the Sea of Hoolemere and the island became the Island of Hoole. And it was in the Great Ga'Hoole Tree that the king lived with his queen, Emerilla, and together they grew old.

Then one day, King Hoole said to Emerilla, "I have something to tell you."

"I know, Hoole," she said quietly.

"You know? How is that, my dear? What do you know?"

"I know it is time to take the ember back to Beyond the Beyond."

"Yes. I promised Grank I would do this when he lay on his deathbed, but I would have done it, anyway. The magic is too powerful even for our own sons and daughters, who are strong and noble of gizzard. It is simply too dangerous to leave in this world. It must be buried in one of the volcanoes."

And so, telling no one, the two elderly Spotted Owls who now were almost as white as Snowies flew without ceremony or escort from the island across the Sea of Hoolemere to Beyond the Beyond. And when they got there, an ancient wolf was waiting.

"Namara!" Hoole hooted.

"Yes, Hoole." Beside her stood the offspring of those wolves who had fought at the Battle of the Ice Palace. "Many of these wolves are MacDuncans, pups of those who fought so valiantly in the Battle of the Ice Palace and kin of Duncan who killed Kreeth. They will keep watch on the ring of the volcanoes, to guard the ember for that owl whose destiny it is to retrieve. Among themselves they have decided to call the chief of their watch Fengo."

Hoole blinked, and in that blink so many memories

flooded back to him — his earliest days on the island in the Bitter Sea, Grank's passionate care for him, the lessons he learned from Fengo, his friends — Phineas, Theo, the Snow Rose, whose great-granddaughter now sang for the tree. What a life he had led.

Hoole spread his wings and lofted into the air. He carried the ember — not in the teardrop container that Theo had made for him — but in his talons as he first had carried it when he retrieved it from the volcano of H'rathmore. All the volcanoes began to erupt in a fury, and the sky was scorched with their flames and, in the flames, images began to emerge. Hoole could see a patch of white and two coal-black eyes. A Barn Owl? Yes, definitely a Barn Owl. But hundreds of years, maybe a thousand years from now. He let the ember drop into the flaming mouth of a volcano. He watched as the ember, with its lick of blue at the center surrounded by the green of a wolf's eyes, sparkled, then winked and was gone, swallowed by the bubbling lava.

But a Barn Owl will come . . .

Or so we believe, but by that time I who have told this tale shall be long gone to glaumora.

Epilogue

Soren closed the final book of legends. There was silence among the six owls. The ember in the latticed iron box glowed as fiercely as ever.

"He returned it to the volcano," Coryn whispered in disbelief, and then turned to his uncle Soren. "And so must I."

"Not yet. Your work is not done," Soren replied. "Indeed, it is only just begun."

"But it is so dangerous." Coryn opened his eyes wide, stared at the ember, and then blinked rapidly as if he could not quite believe how dangerous this thing was that glowed in its lattice box.

"Coryn, you're the Barn Owl that Hoole saw in the flames of the volcano," Digger spoke firmly. "It is your destiny."

"You must fight for it, Coryn," Twilight added.

"It is not only a question of power," Gylfie said. "It is also one of character. You have the character, Coryn, to

resist the bad influences of the ember — the nachtmagen — and use it for good things."

"And the nachtmagen must be gone now," Twilight
added. "It died with the last hagsfiend — centuries ago."

Coryn felt a deep and awful tremor seize his gizzard.
An almost palpable anxiety stirred the air.

"What is it, Coryn?" Otulissa came over and gently
began to preen his flight feathers.

"Nothing . . . nothing," Coryn said, and cast a quick
glance at Soren. But there was something. Between the
uncle and nephew, there was a dark, unspeakable secret.
For the two owls suspected that not all nachtmagen had
died. That the last hagsfiend had not died and through
her, nachtmagen lived on.

OWLS
and others from the

GUARDIANS OF GA'HOOLE SERIES

The Band

SOREN: Barn Owl, *Tyto alba*, from the Forest Kingdom of Tyto; escaped from St. Aegolius Academy for Orphaned Owls; a Guardian at the Great Ga'Hoole Tree

GYLFIE: Elf Owl, *Micranthene whitneyi*, from the Desert Kingdom of Kuneer; escaped from St. Aegolius Academy for Orphaned Owls; Soren's best friend; a Guardian at the Great Ga'Hoole Tree

TWILIGHT: Great Gray Owl, *Strix nebulosa*, free flier; orphaned within hours of hatching; Guardian at the Great Ga'Hoole Tree

DIGGER: Burrowing Owl, *Athene cunicularia*, from the Desert Kingdom of Kuneer; lost in the desert after attack in which his brother was killed by owls from St. Aegolius; a Guardian at the Great Ga'Hoole Tree

The Leaders of the Great Ga'Hoole Tree

CORYN: Barn Owl, *Tyto alba*, the new young king of the great tree; son of Nyra, leader of the Pure Ones

EZYLRYB: Whiskered Screech Owl, *Otus trichopsis*, the wise old weather-interpretation and colliering ryb (teacher) at the Great Ga'Hoole Tree; Soren's mentor (also known as LYZE OF KIEL)

Others at the Great Ga'Hoole Tree

OTULISSA: Spotted Owl, *Strix occidentalis*, a student of prestigious lineage at the Great Ga'Hoole Tree

OCTAVIA: Kielian snake, nest-maid for many years for Madame Plonk and Ezylryb (also known as BRIGID)

Characters from the Time of the Legends

GRANK: Spotted Owl, *Strix occidentalis*, the first collier; friend to young King H'rath and Queen Siv during their youth; first owl to find the ember

H'RATH: Spotted Owl, *Strix occidentalis*, King of the N'yrthghar, a frigid region known in later times as the Northern Kingdoms; father of Hoole

SIV: Spotted Owl, *Strix occidentalis*, mate of H'rath and Queen of the N'yrthghar, a frigid region known in later times as the Northern Kingdoms; mother of Hoole

JOSS: Whiskered Screech, *Otus trichopsis*, loyal, able messenger; served under King H'rath, then under Hoole

LORD RATHNIK: Whiskered Screech, *Otus trichopsis*, officer of the Ice Regiment and member of parliament at the great tree

LORD ARRIN: Spotted Owl, *Strix occidentalis*, traitorous chieftain of a kingdom bordering King H'rath's realm; killed H'rath

PLEEK: Great Horned Owl, *Bubo virginianus*, enemy of King H'rath; known to consort with hagsfiends and to have taken one, Ygryk, for a mate

THEO: Great Horned Owl, *Bubo virginianus*, a gizzard-resister and apprentice to Grank; possesses great blacksmithing skills

SHADYK: Great Horned Owl, *Bubo virginianus*, Theo's brother; mad usurper of King H'rath's throne in the Ice Palace

STRIX STRUMAJEN: Spotted Owl, *Strix occidentalis*, appointed by Hoole to be teacher of first weathering chaw; mother of Emerilla

EMERILLA: Spotted Owl, *Strix occidentalis*, daughter of Strix Strumajen; excellent fighter with the short blade; thought to be lost in a skirmish over the Ice Fangs

SVENKA: Polar Bear in the Bitter Sea; comes to the aid of Queen Siv

SVARR: Polar bear, father of Svenka's cubs; listener at smee holes

PENRYCK: Male hagsfiend, ally of Lord Arrin

YGRYK: Female hagsfiend, Pleek's mate

KREETH: Female hagsfiend with strong powers of nacht-magen; friend of Ygryk; conjures Lutta into being

LUTTA: Female hagsfiend with powers of transformation conjured by Kreeth; takes the form of Emerilla

ULLRYCK: Female hagsfiend, deadly assassin in Lord Arrin's service

PHINEAS: Pygmy Owl, *Glaucidium californicum*, friend of Hoole and owl of great pluck

THE SNOW ROSE: Snowy Owl, *Bubo scandiacus*, gadfeather and renowned singer; joins fight against Lord Arrin; comes to the great tree with Hoole

DUNLEAVY MACHEATH: dire wolf; leader of the MacHeath clan and enemy of Fengo

NAMARA MACNAMARA: dire wolf; former member of MacHeath clan; kills Dunleavy MacHeath, her former mate; joins Hoole at the Battle of the Short Light and Long Night

"Y ou are worried that kings shouldn't just have fun?" Soren blinked at his nephew.

"Well, I don't want to be thought of as ..." He hesitated.

"A sporting king?"

"I suppose so, yes."

"But," Soren said eagerly now, "even a king must be curious about how the hard-won peace lies on the land. These are exciting times."

"It is a good plan, Uncle!" Coryn spoke now with genuine enthusiasm. "But we should meet with the Band to discuss it first, don't you think?"

"Yes, of course," Soren agreed. "We'll speak with them immediately and the parliament must be consulted on the morrow. First Black."

"And Otulissa, will she come as well?" Coryn asked. Otulissa, although considered by many a prickly sort with a confidence bordering on arrogance, was a favorite of Coryn's. Otulissa was the first Guardian of Ga'Hoole that Coryn had met. Through some scroomish vision, an odd phenomenon in itself for an owl who was so dedicated to rational thought, Otulissa had been inspired to go to the Beyond. It was there she encountered Coryn and seemed instantly to sense his destiny and that she was part of it. It was Otulissa, the prodigiously talented and knowledge-able Spotted Owl, who first taught Coryn to dive for coals. She claimed no credit, however, for Coryn had a remark-able genius for colliering and in no time had learned to pluck the most challenging of coals from the volcanoes' spume — the bonk ones that many colliers never learned to retrieve.

"I doubt if Otulissa, with her additional responsibili-ties, will be able to accompany us," Soren said. "But I shall certainly ask her."

Otulissa, an esteemed teacher of the tree, had recently been appointed chief ryb, as her expertise extended over so many of the disciplines — from the literature of the legends to the sciences, including weather interpretation and metals. She hardly had a moment to spare. Nonetheless Soren would go to the hollow where she resided with her old nest-maid snake, Audrey, to ask if she would travel with them. But first he would meet with Gylfie, Twilight, and Digger. And, of course, he would have to explain to Pelli. No doubt Basha, Blythe, and Bell would beg Soren to wait until they had fledged their flight feathers so they might go, too. But they were at least a moon cycle away from fledging, and this was not a trip for young'uns.

Soren was just about to leave the hollow, immensely pleased with himself for coming up with this idea, when Coryn suddenly said, "Uncle?"

"Yes?"

"What about the ember?"

"The ember? What about it?" Soren asked, slightly bewildered.

"Will it be safe here?"

"I can't imagine a safer place than here in the great tree. We certainly don't want to carry it around with us." He paused and looked steadily at the ember. In a low voice he said, "We do not want to become slaves to the ember. If the legends taught us anything, it was that."

"You are right, Uncle. We are free owls!"

Out past the reach of the Ga'Hoole Tree, where survival is the only law, live the Wolves of the Beyond.

New from Kathryn Lasky

WOLVES OF THE BEYOND

In the harsh wilderness beyond Ga'Hoole, a wolf mother hides in fear. Her newborn pup has a twisted paw. The mother knows the rigid rules of her kind. The pack cannot have weakness. Her pup must be abandoned—condemned to die. But the pup, Faolan, does the unthinkable. He survives. This is his story—the story of a wolf pup who rises up to change forever the Wolves of the Beyond.

SCHOLASTIC

www.scholastic.com

WOLVES